SHATTERED LIGHT

UNIVERSAL WILDERNESS: BOOK TWO

FREDRICK NILES

FEVER GARDEN PUBLISHING

Copyright © 2020 by Fredrick Niles

All rights reserved.

No part of this book may be reproduced in any form or by any electronic or mechanical means, including information storage and retrieval systems, without written permission from the author, except for the use of brief quotations in a book review.

SHATTERED LIGHT

First edition. August 7, 2020.

ISBN: 978-1-950021-09-3

Fever Garden Publishing

Cover design by

TheCoverCollection.com

❀ Created with Vellum

"The control of information is something the elite always does, particularly in a despotic form of government. Information, knowledge, is power. If you can control information, you can control people."

— TOM CLANCY

"The Light shines in the darkness, and the darkness did not comprehend it."

— JOHN 1:5 (NASB)

PROLOGUE

Seamus Clark, the Minister of Defense for the People's Union Coalition, sat in a sparsely furnished room with twenty-five other officials for the weekly Strategic Planning meeting. They all sat around a long grey table with the brand new reclining chairs that had recently replaced the aluminum ones after the last budget was pushed through and Clark noticed that the tone in the room had very quickly jumped from hostile to friendly and was now easing back into hostile.

It was absolutely preposterous that the quality of seating was something he had to consider when submitting proposals but here he was. Naturally, there were far greater variables to consider—public awareness of the riots in the Onyx System, opportunities for funding, and the President's approval rating for starters—but in his nineteen years of experience as Minister of Defense, he had learned that mood decided everything. He had learned that his proposals were received more positively in the afternoon after people had already eaten lunch and weren't prone to the irritation of hunger. Mondays were best for Strategic

Planning meetings because everyone in this room was a schemer at heart, and schemers didn't like to have to alter their plans halfway through the week. Then, most importantly, young ambitious senators with their *I'm the only one who can save the universe* attitude were easy to lead around by leaking information to the media and gaming public opinion, while the slovenly comfort-protecting old guard could be manipulated by leaking new information to them directly and allowing them to assert their relevance.

As far as today's proposal was concerned, he would be pursuing the old guard. He had already won a few of the younger senators over by convincing them that the Pillon System was a backwoods cesspool of separatist rhetoric that needed to be bolted shut and shoveled full of dirt if they wanted to stop the riots in the Onyx System and regain political control. Violent race-based crimes had been occurring more and more frequently, and if they wanted to clamp a lid on it they'd have to stem the flow of information from that area.

So now he'd be pursuing the older bureaucrats that had an ax to grind with the Pillon System and wanted that thorn-in-the-side removed before they retired. And that was the key: young politicians would ignore the truth for the sake of ideals while old politicians would outright lie for the sake of settling old grievances. And the Pillon System had certainly racked up their fair share of grievances with elected officials.

Today he'd be focusing on getting this proposal pushed through with this room of babbling ingrates, most of whom comprised the old guard. So his strategy would be to exploit their sensitivity to time.

"The Pillon System is the last system existing outside of the net," he said, addressing the room. "Most of their communication is word-of-mouth and we all know how reliable that is. So not only are they constantly misinformed about current events but they then *spread* that misinformation back into the other systems. Normally this wouldn't be a problem, but the public's attitude toward the Pillon System is steadily tilting away from them being a *quaint outer colony* and towards them being a breeding ground for separatist sentiments. Most influential public figures think we're already dragging our feet on implementing regulations and have begun to blame Pillon for the riots and ideologically motivated crimes in the Onyx System. So if we can launch a blitz attack—get in there *fast* and *hard*—and get a Light Wire up and running before news of the action begins to filter out by word-of-mouth then we can count the operation as a victory towards progress and hopefully get the Onyx System under control before the next election cycle." Clark leaned back in his new office chair. "But the clock is ticking here guys. The situation in Onyx is unstable and if we don't get this under control now, then who knows what it'll look like in a few months."

"Doesn't it take a long time to build a Light Wire installation?" asked a willowy white-haired man named Bick Johnson. Johnson was the Secretary of the Treasury, and while Clark would have liked his approval, it probably mattered the least of all.

"I have a group of operatives on the ground on Desia who have already built the installation inside of an abandoned iron refinery. All we need to do now is switch it on."

Clark was proud of that. Getting operatives who could be both trusted and discreet onto a planet like Desia was no easy task, and then smuggling in all of the materials necessary for the construction of the Light Wire had been monumental in itself. Over the last few years, tiny pieces of equipment had to be slowly filtered in shipments of building supplies through a non-regulated company who took fistfuls of cash under the table and—by the time this was all done—a few well-placed energy bolts to the head.

That was for later, though. Right now, Clark just had to get the Wire up and running.

The Light Wire was something of a new technology that used Light Cores to instantly transmit information to other Light Wire Facilities and Light Cores, which could then transmit to any station in-system. Light Cores were rare and required special circuit grounding to contain. They were also what allowed ships to travel through Void Gates.

People still had a few Tesla Arcs tucked away, which were the previous form of Void navigation hardware, but most had been confiscated when the People's Union Coalition or PUC had outlawed all private Void travel. Most of the arcs had then been repurposed to power the onboard weapons systems for the PUC's naval fleet. Now, the only ships left that could legally jump from system to system were logistical, military, and public transit vessels. All of these were closely screened and anyone trying to travel without the correct authorization would be detained without trial under the Union Protection Act, one of Seamus Clark's greatest achievements. The UPA had cut down violent crime numbers by over 60%, owing mostly to the heavy restrictions on unregulated travel. It also gave law enforcement officials strict quotas and an ambitious violent crime rate threshold that they couldn't exceed without losing funding.

That wasn't what Minister Clark was focused on now, however. What interested him now was the final and most important goal of his career: the control of information.

Each Light Wire facility was owned and operated by the

PUC government, which meant that nothing could pass through it without being given the "okay" by a censorship official. Most people didn't realize it but the PUC's biggest war wasn't fought with energy bolts or Tesla Arc bombardments but with information. Information and misinformation created civil unrest and led to riots, hate crimes, and generally misinformed voters. Even things like robbery and assault fell under Clark's jurisdiction, so if he could manufacture systematic solutions to those by getting the right people in office then he'd be saving millions of lives.

And the Pillon System was the last refuge for separatist sympathizers that would rather bury their heads in the sand and play a deadly game of telephone with vital facts and news. If Clark could secure Pillon, then he could secure every planetary system under PUC control.

"If it's as easy as throwing a switch," said Vice President Kurtz, a heavyset man with sharp blue eyes, "then why don't you just do that? Why do we need to bust down their door?"

"Because it would be taken down almost immediately," Clark said, trying not to lose his patience. "Desian authorities would have an armed response team on the premises in under ten minutes and from there all they would have to do is rig up a few pounds of C4 to bring it down. Plus, if we can get in there fast enough, I'd like to broker a deal with those in charge. If we can have televised images of the Light Wire going up *with* their endorsement, then that could go a long way."

"A deal?" Kurtz scoffed. "Desia barely *has* any authorities. You'll be shaking hands with some powerless shell of a figure."

"So to be clear," President Richard Cole interrupted from his spot at the head of the table. Clark watched the man recline in his new chair with just a twinge of satisfaction. "You are proposing an *attack*? Not a political takeover but a full-scale naval invasion. Am I correct?"

Clark nodded. "I am. I suspect there will be some level of casualties and general loss of life, but weigh that against the long-term security and stability of an entire interplanetary system and I think you'll see the math works *heavily* in our favor."

"Mmmhmmm." The President looked down at the table. "Will you be using combat synthetics or PUC personnel?"

"PUC personnel," Clark answered without hesitation. "Synths won't be good for much other than standing guard after all of the fighting is over. Now, it should be over relatively *quickly,* I should add, but the point is: this attack is going to be absolutely crushing and overwhelming. But I'm not looking for a bloodbath. I need control, not dead bodies."

"And what if public opinion changes? What if our actions in the Pillon System are seen as an aggressive act of imperialism?"

Clark shook his head emphatically. "This is progress, not imperialism. Imperialism is what happened before the People's Union Coalition was formed. If anything, what these separatist fascists are doing is imperialistic. They're holdovers of an inherently oppressive structure that was founded in conquering new worlds through force and domination. What we're doing is eliminating any vestige of that. And with the Light Wire we can get on top of all news and dissemination of information. There will be the occasional conspiracy theory, sure, but those sources have already cried wolf so many times that it would almost be suspicious if they didn't."

"And if something does leak? Say one of your Marauders guns down a civilian in the streets and someone takes a video of it and spreads it around to their friends? Then their friends spread it to their friends and so on?"

Anger flashed through Clark's head and he hoped it didn't show on his face. "Marauder" was a slang term for the Surgical Equalizing Unit Program he had worked on as a General with the former Minister of Defense. Whenever someone in this room used the word, it was almost certainly derogatory. On more than one occasion, Clark had considered submitting a proposal for the term to be put on the banned speech list as it undermined the public's opinion of his special forces assets and thus, endangered the lives of the people he was trying to protect. In effect, the word was an act of literal violence.

"Video footage can be easily fabricated these days," Clark replied, filtering the scorn from his voice. "There are already hundreds of those videos floating around, all of them forgeries. Evidence isn't proof of anything anymore. It's just political ammunition."

"That's what I'm worried about. What if our political opponents get ahold of it?"

"I don't think you're understanding me," Clark said, then immediately regretted it. "I see your concern: you're worried about this operation undermining our credibility. But if I may speak honestly, I've spent *years* pouring over footage that has been released from the Pillon System and let me assure you of this: there's so much of that shit coming out of there already that it would just be white noise." He held up a hand. "Pardon the language."

"I see," the President said. "You're actively trying to *stop* harmful information from being disseminated, not provide another opportunity for it to be created?"

"Yes, sir." Clark nodded and was pleased when he saw the lights turn on in a number of other people's faces. Most had just been slowly nodding along, likely running over their own proposals, but now he had their attention. The President got it, and if they could get in on the ground floor quickly enough, then they could share in the glory.

"So how many vessels are we thinking here?" asked Martha Ramiriz, the Commissioner for Defense Contracts.

Clark answered all of their questions while the President leaned back in his chair. The time was about 13:00 and a few of the officials at the table had joined President Cole for a private lunch prior to the meeting. Clark watched with satisfaction as Cole's eyelids grew heavy, the comfort of the room seeping into his very bones.

———

WHEN SEVENTEEN-YEAR-OLD LUCAS CLARK'S father got home from work he rushed to meet him at the door. Waking up this morning, he had known that today was the day—today was the first official step towards a peaceful universe. Soon, they'd be on Desia in the Pillon System and then the Light Wire would be switched on. And then?

And then the entire universe would be connected by one network.

"How was work?" Lucas asked his father, almost breathless. He had asked the same question every day for the last two weeks. He knew that his father would be proposing action on Desia soon, but not how soon.

"Went well," his father answered, facing away as he hung up his coat. Lucas tried to read him.

"Anything of note?" He prodded.

"Nothing I can talk about." His father turned around, a big smile on his face, and Lucas knew. The man before him practically radiated pride.

"Could it be related to a certain planet in the Pillon System? Maybe, about dragging it into the modern age?" The question was brazen. Lucas hadn't intended on asking it outright, but he needed to know. Needed confirmation.

His father visibly blanched. A look of worry etched itself into his lined face and Lucas was quick to deflect scrutiny.

"It is, isn't it?" He said. He slapped his knee. "I knew it. As soon as you walked in the door, I knew it. You've been working on something for *months*. Very secretive."

"What makes you think it's about Desia?"

"Simple process of elimination," he answered, turning around on the couch. He was a good liar, but his dad was good at rooting out the truth. Better to hide his face. "You've been trying to lock down the flow of rhetoric from Pillon for years. That independent journalist on Desia just inspired a hate crime on the Onyx System. You've got probable cause now. Public opinion is turning in your favor. It was just a matter of time, really."

The truth was that, in the dark pre-dawn hours of a day almost two years ago, Lucas had overheard his dad speaking with someone on the phone. Peering over the top of the stairs, Lucas had strained to hear the words his father was issuing forth into a small black burner phone he had never seen before. Lucas hadn't been able to pick up much, but he had gleaned enough. Something about secretly shipping equipment into hostile territory. It could have been any number of conflict-ridden planets within PUC space, but Lucas didn't think so. The level of secrecy. His father's body language and voice. It had all pointed at something bigger. Something grand.

The final move in a long game of chess. The endgame.

Ever since that night, Lucas had paid close attention to the tiny breadcrumbs his father had dropped in passing conversation. A hint of something here. An off-comment there.

Lucas had no real proof of his father's plan other than the fact that one day, almost four years ago, he had suggested it himself. With the unsophisticated mind of a 12-year-old child, Lucas had come right out and said it, "Why not just invade Desia and build a Light Wire."

His father had laughed the idea off, claiming that the reality of the situation was much more complicated. The Pillon System wasn't some toothless population eager to step into the light of modernity. They were a hodgepodge of reckless, often violent militias. Possessing very little overarching structure, the five planets that made up the system practically thrummed with a taste for violence. That, and the planets' geographies were well-suited for guerrilla warfare. The PUC could invade and secure them easily enough, but could they hold them?

Seamus Clark had explained all of this to Lucas, and Lucas hadn't argued. Instead, he had kept the coals of that conversation hot. Over the years, they had revisited the topic and Lucas had perceived a noticeable shift in his father's demeanor. He had gone from being skeptical to theoretical planning. What *if* they could secure a Light Wire on Desia?

Eventually, his father had begun talking about the act as if it were possible. And that's when Lucas knew. Even before he had overheard the conversation, he had suspected that things were in motion. Small, secretive steps. But steps nonetheless.

And now, they had reached the final lap. The finish line was in sight.

"I will neither confirm nor deny," his father said, smiling. He walked into the kitchen and opened the fridge. "A proposal like that might sound a little wild, but Harris submitted her proposal for synthetic rights for the umpteenth time today and in light of that, a proposal to put a Light Wire on Desia might suddenly seem reasonable." He closed the fridge with a can of beer in his hand and snapped the tab open.

Lucas laughed. "I take it hers got shot-down then?"

"Well, they threw her a bone," he said. "They said they'd push it through on a planetary level on some of the Onyx planets and see how it does there."

"Ah, so that way there's voter competition between the blue collar workers and the synthetics?" Lucas asked, catching on. Of the Clark family's four children, he was far-and-away the most politically savvy.

His father shot him a wink. "They won't say it but that's almost certainly their reasoning. I don't think they understand what a slippery slope that is though. If goddam *machines* gain voting rights across the universe then our entire infrastructure is at risk. I don't think the everyday person realizes how much of their safe and comfortable lives are upheld by our automated systems."

"I mean, does that mean even *combat synths* would attain citizenship? They could be programmed to vote for *anyone*."

"Pffff," his father plopped down on the couch, loosening his tie. "I don't think they're even thinking about that yet. I think they're just concerned with granting rights to Organic Synthetics." Organic Synthetics were humans that were grown in a lab with organic material. "It's all a voting strate-gy," he said cynically. "If they can grant a bunch of people citizenship then they've just pulled a bunch of voters out of thin air and effectively bought their support."

"That's stupid," Lucas said. He didn't tell his father that in his opinion, the entire voting system was broken anyway. It was all one big popularity contest like at school where the best-looking and most charismatic people thrived, leaving the others to rot in isolation and ridicule. If it were up to him, he'd bring the whole system down to its knees.

Soon, it might be, said a little voice at the back of his mind.

"So when's the day?" he asked. "When do they start building the Light Wire on Desia?" No need to let on that he knew more than he should. In reality, the facility was probably already built.

"We don't have a firm date set," his father said, his tongue beginning to loosen up. He looked over at Lucas. "And no, you can't be there. I know we've been talking about this for a while, but it's just not safe, let alone *legal*. I can't have a minor aboard my ship in the middle of an operation."

Lucas felt his mood dim a bit. He had wanted to be there when the Pillon System finally joined the rest of the world, but no matter. There was a Light Wire here in the capital and he had already secured that location with an internship. His face was so well-known around there that he could basically walk right in and do what he wanted.

"Hey, don't you have Debate Club in an hour?" his dad asked.

"Ugghhhhh," Lucas sighed loudly. "I hate Debate Club. It's just one big group of assholes fighting over who can fart the loudest. And those farts are usually aimed right in the face of logic."

"Hey, language," his father snapped, a little bit of the military disciplinarian coming out. "Now why don't you get on upstairs and get dressed. How do you think your talking points will be received if you're wearing a pair of ripped up jeans and a shirt with cartoons on it," he said, flipping his hand at Lucas's clothes.

"That's the *problem*! It shouldn't-"

"Go!" His father pointed up the stairs.

Without another word, Lucas pounded up the steps and down the hallway to his room. Debate Club was in an hour and it only took 45 minutes to get there and five minutes to get dressed, so he didn't know what his dad was so concerned about. Not like he'd be welcomed in with open arms anyway, the assholes.

Lucas plopped down on his bed and then looked over at the wide-range receiver he had built sitting at the desk currently serving as his nightstand. He had modeled the receiver after the blueprints of the Light Wire he had downloaded at the library. Obviously, he couldn't get ahold of an actual Light Core to use, but he had been building miniature Tesla coils since he was a child in Science Club, and had been able to boost the receiver's range and capabilities almost up to that of the comm systems his dad's SEUs used. The real break had come however, when he had found a virtual backdoor into the Light Wire after his internship had started and he was able to piggyback on its signal.

Now, to do what Lucas was planning on doing, he'd need direct access to the Light Wire. That wasn't much of a problem but he had been hoping he could do it on Desia when it went live, if for no other reason than to see the look on his father's face.

It was irrelevant in the end though. What would be done would be done and all that mattered was that it happened at all. Who knows, he thought, maybe he'd even be able to bring his receiver with and talk to his dad directly. He'd be changing the wavelength of the Light Wire but that shouldn't matter. He should still be able to communicate over it. Wasn't that the whole point?

Lucas stood up and walked around to his desk. He

reached down and picked up the receiver and toggled the switch.

At first, there was nothing, as there always was. Just a light hiss of static over placid silence. He had found the signal one day while systematically going through channel-by-channel. Then, there it was.

Light Cores and Tesla Arcs honed in on light spectrums that were more similar to spacial coordinates than classic radio frequencies. This allowed for both sound and matter to travel over incalculable distances VIA gates to the Void Dimension, a plane of existence where space seemed to exist but not time. In the early days when humanity was beginning to explore space, they used these coordinates to travel from Void Gate to Void Gate, allowing them access to star systems.

In those early days of exploration, they would run long sequences of coordinates, sending a ping to each one, and if they got a ping back, then that meant there was a Void Gate they could travel through.

Most of the old channels had been forgotten by now, but one day Lucas had been scanning them anyway, just to see if any strange sounds came across. He remembered the first time he heard the signal with extreme vividness. That seemingly empty airwave that shouldn't and technically *couldn't* be used to transmit sound.

He hadn't even been able to tell when it started, so soft it had come in, but after a few minutes, it was there. Strong. Clear.

And alien.

He slowly realized that what he was listening to was *music*. The seemingly random notes that began to coalesce into something bigger. Something *wider*. Lucas had spent hours listening to the steady *gulp-gulp* sound of the bass, as if it was made by something swallowing. He had listened to it and understood it—understood what it meant —what it *could* mean. Not in words, but in his body. In his soul.

Then one day his father had come home talking about Desia and the Pillon System again and how they still couldn't stem the tide of rhetoric being espoused by its inhabitants. That's when a solution had clicked in Lucas's brain.

Not a solution to the information distribution problem he had hashed over so many times with his father, but to everything. To humanity. The idea had dropped down into his mind almost as if it had been planted like a seed from some foreign hand.

The Light Wire. Connection to all of PUC controlled space. The song he had heard. The sheer scale and implications of it rattled his heart and shook his soul.

The whole world in the palm of his hands. The PUC had thought they were creating a network of information all of these years. A safety net. A wall of security that hedged against undesirable rhetoric.

But what they had actually created was a steering wheel. And once the final piece was in place, all that was needed was for someone to reach out and grab it.

Lucas thought about planting the final Light Wire on Desia—remembered watching the idea quickly take hold in his father's mind, transforming from his son's idea into his own. Now it was all finally coming together, the future descending upon the present.

He could already see everyone's faces as they realized what he had done—the looks of shock and horror when they realized that the insignificant little mote they knew as Lucas Clark was actually capable of creating quite a bit of noise. There were the larger considerations of course, like the ultimate fate of the entire known universe for example, but that was inevitable anyway. And who said you couldn't enjoy bringing peace to all of existence?

Truth be told, he didn't know what form it would take. Not really. All he knew was the song. The gap it would fill. The revelation of it all.

The Crimson Coronach. That's what it was called. He wasn't sure where that name had come from but there it was, up in his head like a drifter blowing in from the cold.

Lucas leaned back, letting the music play. It was beautiful, really. It had sounded ugly at first but it was the ugliness that he had connected with. And it wasn't that it was convincing him to *do* anything really. It was more that it was just so simple and complete. And if he could only make people hear it, then they would be able to see something that only he saw. Feel something that only he felt. Soon the whole universe would know him. Know his will. His *intent*.

Soon, they would see what only he could see.

1

THE VOID TUNNEL

"We're coming up on it," 49 said from the pilot's seat of the Leopold. It wasn't *exactly* a pilot's "seat," as they had had to remove the chair itself to be able to wire 49 into the bridge's conduit system. The ship could still fly without the android plugged in the way he was, but due to the Light Core he currently housed inside of his body, he was required for both Void navigation and their heavy weapon's system. Both of which they were about to need.

"What's this thing gonna look like?" Byzzie asked from the gunner's seat. "Am I even going to be able to know what to shoot at?"

"Don't shoot at *anything* yet," 49 warned. He was steering the ship smoothly toward what looked like a giant solar storm, arcs of lightning cutting across the black. "There are things in there that won't even glance at being hit by a Javelin round." The Javelin was the ship's heavy artillery.

"Yeah, well, I'm not taking any risks," Captain Ritz said from the captain's seat. "If something looks at us sideways I'm giving it a new mouth."

"There are creatures in the Void Tunnel that—if you were to shoot them—would literally grow a new mouth," 49 said. "And you don't want those to have any more mouths than they already do."

Trapped in a system with no Void Gate to travel through, the Leopold had been stranded after a botched jump almost three weeks ago. Since then, they had been lured onboard a marooned two-century-old ghost ship by a deranged AI system, fought indescribable horrors, lost their pilot, and then replaced their lost pilot with the deranged AI after defeating him and altering his bio-mechanical make-up with the Light Core. They had also *hopefully* changed his views on being murderous and deranged.

Byzzie wasn't so sure however, and though she was glad she could have 49 upfront to keep an eye on, she wasn't exactly thrilled about giving him the wheel of the ship. She looked back at Ritz and saw that the captain shared the same concern.

"Just know," Byzzie said. "If you're leading us into some sort of trap, I have the override controls to the ship right here in front of me. And even if we can't escape with our lives, I can turn that Light Core in your belly into a really *bright* Light Core, if you catch my meaning. Then you'll just be a smudge of golden dust on the asshole of the universe. Got it?"

"For the 11th time, I-" the android raised his hands and made a pair of quotation marks with his metallic fingers, "-'got it.'"

Byzzie looked back toward the viewport of the ship. "I don't think you're using those right."

"I'm *trying* to use them to navigate through a wormhole in space," he explained.

"I was talking about the quot-"

"Shove a cork in it, Byzzie," Ritz said irritably. "This is our only way back and I don't want the ship to crash and explode because you were too busy fighting with the nav-system."

Byzzie ground her teeth and looked at 49 who threw her a wry smile, causing her to grind them even harder. She didn't like that he was playing games with her.

"Again," Byzzie said, trying to keep her voice serene, "what exactly is this thing going to look like?"

"It's going to look like you're flying through a storm," 49 said. "Then it's going to look like—well, you'll see."

Byzzie pursed her lips and shot a glance back at the captain, who was willfully ignoring her. *You're lucky this bucket doesn't have an eject-button, buddy,* she muttered to herself. 49 didn't answer but she thought she may have caught him smirking.

The ship jostled and rocked as they entered the storm. The viewport became obscured and they soon had to switch to instrumental navigation. Another flash of lightning cracked the sky in front of them.

"It feels like this thing is going to come apart," Byzzie yelled over the racket. "Are you sure we can handle it?"

"I am not," 49 said, increasing his volume. "I barely made it through with the Mary when I got excommunicated from the Void. So who knows what it looks like at this point." Mary's Burden had been the ghost ship they found the android on.

"Focus," Ritz yelled, stretching out the word. "I'm not seeing barriers on the imaging screen but that doesn't mean there aren't any. Plus, I imagine getting hit by one of those lightning strikes wouldn't end very well for us."

They careened through the storm, avoiding the rough patches as best they could. At one point, a fork of lightning streaked so close to the window that they were all temporarily blinded, a white fuzz hanging in their vision as an electrical buzz permeated the whole bridge.

Another fork flared farther off. It wasn't close enough to harm them but what it illuminated was.

"*Holy shit,*" Ritz yelled. "What is *that*?" A giant whale-like shape loomed in the murk, its enormous silhouette outlined by the lightning.

"Don't worry," 49 said. "It's just here to feed off of the storm. There are some creatures that live off of direct energy alone."

"Yeah, I'm more worried about running into it," Byzzie said. "Anyone got eyes on it?" She searched for the massive shape which had once again been obscured by the darkness.

"My instruments are picking it up," 49 replied. "It's off to the right, moving left at a 314-degree angle." He tapped at the keyboard. "Banking right and down."

The ship veered down and though they couldn't see it, Byzzie thought she could feel an eerie crackle pass over her head as they descended. The nose of the Leopold leveled out again and continued on through the storm.

They picked up two more of the creatures on their sensors, catching a glimpse of one of them, and 49 gave them a wide berth as he pushed forward. A few more lightning strikes crashed and then all at once, the rumbling in the ship ceased as the space in front of them cleared and opened up to reveal a dense purple-tinged expanse of things so bizarre that they defied everything and anything Byzzie had ever experienced in her time aboard spacecraft.

Giant globules of magenta liquid pulsed, separated, and merged together in front of them. Off to the sides were huge lily pad-like structures that a menagerie of bizarre and impossible creatures occupied. One of them looked vaguely cat-like with a heavy mane of translucent bristles while another moved like some combination of an octopus and a tree-frog, alternating between hopping and swimming.

"What is this place?" Byzzie said with amazement. She could feel her jaw hanging open but didn't care.

"Whenever a tunnel is bored out of or into the Void," 49 explained, "it creates a unique environment populated by any number of non-atmospheric dependent life-forms. Occasionally, a tunnel like this one will open up and energy from the Void will transform whatever particles get caught inside into-" he gestured at the viewport "-something like this."

"Are you saying that you didn't create this tunnel?" Ritz asked.

The android shook his head. "When I was jettisoned out of the Void, I fell into a slipstream that led me here. Some openings into the Void are clean and neat like the Void Gates, while others are closer to gradual transitions like these."

"What causes them?" Byzzie asked, her attention focused on what she had thought was some sort of large stalk-like plant but which ended up sprouting fins out of its side and swimming away like a long, skinny fish.

"No one knows for sure. But almost everything you see here was created at the time of the Dislocation." The Dislocation was a massive cosmic event that had suddenly and inexplicably scattered humanity across the universe, resulting in countless deaths and—apparently—tears in the fabric of space and time that took the form of Void Gates and Tunnels.

Suddenly, the ship rocked and halted its progression onward.

"What the fuck was that?" Ritz said, freezing in place.

Both 49 and Byzzie hurriedly scrolled and tapped through their counsels, trying to discern the problem. Finally, Byzzie pulled up a view screen from a camera mounted on the back of the ship. "That doesn't look good," she said.

Up from somewhere down below them, a long cord of *something* had emerged to fasten itself to the back of the ship.

"What is it?" The captain leaned in. "I can't tell if it's from a plant or an animal."

"Those distinctions don't always hold in these environments," said 49. "Here, let me see if I can burn it off." The ship rocked hard as he swung it sideways, trying to blast the cord with the ship's thrusters. The thrusters fell short and the ship bounced backward again.

As they swung back around however, trying to build up momentum so they could pivot far enough sideways, Byzzie noticed that the cloud of purple haze the cord was coming from was growing darker. She squinted and leaned in to look at the view screen.

"Jesus, we need to move," she said suddenly. 49 swung the ship for a second time and once again the thrusters fell short.

Two rows of sharp, serrated teeth had appeared above and below the area where the cord was coming from and seemed to be rushing quickly toward them.

Byzzie punched at her counsel and brought the Leopold's ballistic defense system online. Unlike the Javelin and Chopper systems that were hooked into 49's Light Core, the ship's old defense system used good-old-fashioned machine gun rounds. She turned the left toggle in front of her, trying to get a lock on what must have been the advancing creature's tongue. She failed, trying in-turn to get a lock on the creature itself, but it was approaching almost directly from the rear, which was the ship's blind spot in terms of defenses.

"Forget the ballistics," Ritz said hurriedly. "Fire up the Javelin."

Byzzie punched some keys and just as the Javelin came online, the ship rocked one last time as 49 swung the thrusters, this time successfully frying the creature's tongue off.

Suddenly, the massive shape of a predatory fish-like creature rocketed passed on the left, just barely missing them. "Hit it!" Ritz yelled as Byzzie's targeting indicators secured a lock.

Byzzie pulled the big red trigger on the right-hand toggle and a massive spear of light gushed out of the Javelin barrel on the upper-nose of the ship. The huge fish-like creature was just turning around when the Javelin round hit it behind the eye, blowing it into a hundred different chunks, a cloud of fluorescent orange blood blooming around it.

And then, the Void Tunnel became a jungle of elongated tongues.

"*Go! Go! Go!*" Ritz shouted as 49 slammed the throttle down. The ship blasted forward and then slammed to a halt as another tongue latched onto them. This time though, the Leopold had had enough forward momentum to keep them going, and the ship continued slowly on as if dragging a huge log behind it.

The tongue had latched onto the side of the ship and Byzzie quickly locked onto it with the Leopold's ballistic system and cut it in half with a stream of large-caliber rounds. The ship blasted forward once again.

49 ducked and weaved through the maze of tongues, Byzzie blasting some of them out of the air. The machine guns aboard the Leopold consisted of seven guns along the left-hand-side and seven along the right, amounting to fourteen total. They could each independently lock onto individual targets and as the ship traversed the Void Tunnel its guns seemed to have no lack of those. The bridge purred with the sound of gunfire as countless tongues and their owners were blasted apart around it.

A shape loomed abruptly in front of them and before anyone could react, one of the creature's tongues smacked directly into the bridge's viewport, obscuring their vision. Out of the corner of her eye, Byzzie saw 49 switch to instrumental navigation again and try to bank to the left and then to the right. The ship banked successfully, but was immediately brought back towards the center by the pull of the tongue. Byzzie tried targeting it but before she could the ship plunged into the thing's mouth, all of their auxiliary viewing screens going dark around them. Wasting no time, Byzzie hastily switched the Light Core weapon system from the Javelin to the Chopper and pulled the trigger.

Light strobed in front of them as a long burst of hard light rounds erupted from the ship's Javelin barrel and bored a hole through the creature's body. The giant fish shuttered around them as its long tongue was severed at the connection and it was torn apart from the inside. 49 banked to the right and back at the last second, and the end of the tongue that had affixed itself to the window was effectively wiped off of the viewport as they blasted out the back of the creature in a spray of fluorescent orange fish-guts.

"I can't believe you don't have a pair of windshield wipers on this thing," 49 said.

"Sorry, but navigating through some space-fish's digestive system didn't come up on the list of possible scenarios when I was building mods for the bridge," Byzzie replied. "You can bet your ass they're next on the list though."

The Leopold wove its way through a few more of the giant fish creatures, occasionally blasting one away. The problem was that there were no clearly defined boundaries to the tunnel so it felt as if they were driving in no particular direction, but merely winding their way through a maze of giant space plants and hostile creatures.

"Hey 49, any clue where we're going?" asked Ritz.

"There's an opening to the Void ahead," the android responded. "I'll let you know once we get within range. From there we can jump to the Pillon System."

The Pillon System had been their original destination before running into 49 and the Mary. After engaging a number of PUC vessels that were hell-bent on keeping them from leaving, likely because they had stolen a Light Core and killed a number of people in the process, the crew of the Leopold had taken down a Light Shield blockade that had prevented them from jumping. The Light Shield had been quickly repaired however and when they finally got clear to hit the Void Gate, the shield had come back up at the exact moment Ritz had hit the jump-button, knocking their trajectory off-course.

But now they were *hopefully* back on track, just so long as they could hit the Void and jump to the Pillon System where a number of supporters, including Byzzie's entire extended family waited for them.

Byzzie felt her hope dim however as a large shape loomed in front of them.

"Oh man, I don't like the looks of that," she said as the massive shadow fell over them. The creature was like nothing she had ever seen before. With massive spiny legs coming from all sides, it had the body of a giant slug, the tentacled lower-half of a squid, and the three-jawed mouth of a leech.

Byzzie watched in wonder as one of its sharp-tipped legs abruptly shot out and skewered one of the long-tongued fish. Its leg then swiveled on its body, brought the fish upwards, and finally popped the dead body into its massive mouth.

Ritz suddenly yelled *"shoot it,"* at the same time 49 yelled, *"wait."* Byzzie toggled back to the Javelin and pulled the trigger.

A thick spear of light lanced out from the Javelin barrel, tore through the space in front of them, and then fizzled as it careened into the side of the new monstrosity.

"Hit it again," Ritz yelled frantically.

"I can't," Byzzie said as she locked on with the ballistics system even though she knew it was pointless. "We're dry." And before she could say anymore, one of the creature's legs was piercing the space just above them, 49 managing to put the ship into a controlled dive just in the nick of time.

"Whoa, that was close," Byzzie said as she frantically tried to aim at the leg. Her screen bleeped, letting her know she had secured a lock but she didn't pull the trigger. Shooting it once had already managed to piss it off, so she opted to wait until she had no other choice.

Over the next ten-seconds, Byzzie marveled at the android's lightning-fast reflexes as he avoided stab-after-stab from the thing's legs. Their old pilot Hector never would have been able to pull something like that off, Byzzie thought to herself with a pang of guilt and sadness, and she resented herself for it. After all, the whole reason they were in this mess was because of 49.

"We're almost there," 49 said. "The opening to the Void

is just on the other side of this thing. If we can get around it then we should be close enough to jump."

With every strike however, the creature seemed to be getting closer and closer, as if it was beginning to anticipate their moves. And just when they had almost made their way around the hulking figure, one of the legs knocked into their tail and sent them into a wild spin.

The viewport became a blur as the ship spiraled sideways through space and just when they began to level out they found themselves face-to-face with the monster. The giant slug-like body was bent in half as it lowered its head, its massive jaws separating to take them in. Byzzie depressed the trigger and fourteen jets of tracer-rounds lit up the sky around them as they pelted harmlessly into the creature's side.

Then, just as the jaws came within a stone's throw of the nose of the ship, they began to retreat. Not knowing what had happened at first, Byzzie peered out the viewport to see if she could see anything. And what she saw made her stomach flip.

Something—perhaps "titan" was the word for it—had a massive three-fingered hand wrapped around the monster's midsection. Obscured by clouds and darkness, the arm rose up and out of sight to connect with a creature of which they could only discern the vague outline against the iridescent lights of the Void Tunnel.

The next thing they knew, the big slug-like creature's body was being lowered back down, except now it was lacking a head.

"Get us the fuck *out* of here," Ritz groaned, and as he did 49 pushed the throttle forward. The ship maneuvered down and around the gargantuan trunk of the titan's leg and then the inky blackness of the Void came into view.

Without needing to be told, the android pulled up the coordinates and hit the jump button. And the next thing they knew, the crew aboard the bridge of the Leopold were staring down the barrels of the Pillon System's Orbital Defense Network.

2

DESIA

itz punched in the Leopold's identification code as two defense frigates moved in to block them. Surrounded by a large asteroid belt, the majority of Desia's defenses lay heavily in the stationary defense turrets that had been installed on the orbiting asteroids, but there were still a number of ships they used to guide other vessels to the planet's surface if they were cleared.

The captain waited anxiously as the heavily armed vessels moved in but then the Leopold's comm system blurped and Ritz flipped the switch on his command chair to accept the transmission.

"Civilian Class Vessel designation 'Leopold'," came a stern woman's voice over the comms. "State the purpose of your entry into the Pillon System."

"Nice to see you too, Vanessa," Ritz said. "What's with all of the defenses? Desia seems a little more *prickly* than the last time I was here."

"Captain Riyaad Tariq," the voice said, addressing Ritz by his full name. "I'm going to need a straight answer from you before I even think about telling my vessels to stand down."

"We're wanted by the PUC," he said flatly. "We stole a Light Core from them and are looking for safe haven."

"Desia and the rest of the Pillon System offers safe haven to those ostracized and victimized by the People's Union Coalition. Not to those who willfully antagonize, steal from, and *murder* PUC personnel."

Ritz pursed his lips. In their frantic flight from the PUC facility they had stolen the Light Core from, six security personnel had been accidentally killed not to mention the crews onboard both of the corvettes they had shot down. He had hoped they would reach Desia before the news of their crimes would but apparently their detour through uncharted space had been just long enough to keep that from happening.

"You and I both know you have a massive number of separatist militants on each of the five planets in this system," Ritz said, his voice low. "And I know that *you* know they aren't playing with kid-gloves, so are you going to let us land or what?"

Silence permeated the bridge. Ritz began to drum his fingers on the armrest of his chair. Then finally, Vanessa came back over the line.

"Do you have my daughter onboard, Captain Tariq?"

"I'm here, mom," Byzzie said, toggling the comms. "And I didn't shoot anyone so you can just go ahead and arrest these other criminals if you'd like."

Byzzie's mother didn't say anything, but five seconds later, the defense frigates began to back-off.

"Maybe we should lead with that next time," 49 suggested, but Byzzie was already shaking her head.

"Mom doesn't like it when we play the daughter card.

Sometimes I think she'd just like to forget I'm out here. In fact, I'm pretty sure she tells my aunts and uncles that I'm still out doing PSAs for environmental organizations."

"Why'd you stop doing that?" 49 asked, turning to look at her.

Ritz watched as his gunner mulled that over in her head. Finally, she responded: "Look 49, there's a phrase that you're going to have to get used to if you're going to be walking around down there. So I might as well start conditioning you for it."

"And what's that?"

Byzzie turned to him and met his gaze. "None of your damn business."

———

WHEN RAQUEL FISHER stepped off of the Leopold and onto solid ground, she all but dropped to the dirt and kissed it. She had been watching the ship's progress through the solar storm on her living quarter's view screen, and she had made it a solid two minutes before she had to vomit into the small wastebasket she kept by her bed. She had then felt her stomach lurch after catching a glimpse of the huge leviathans that seemed to inhabit the storm, but she had turned away just in time to keep from throwing up again.

From there, she had been able to cool down as they passed from the storm into the Void Tunnel. She had even admired some of the creatures and structures until they were suddenly thrown right back into the thick of it with those huge predatory fish things. She had really lost it though when the massive titan had reached down and grabbed the other still relatively massive creature that had been blocking their way. Few times in her life had she ever felt so small and helpless and insignificant as in that moment, and she once again hurled into the sloshing bucket, this time, conjuring nothing but a long series of painful dry heaves.

Then, almost immediately after, they had jumped to navigate the Void and Raquel blacked out, which apparently wasn't something that happened to other people. According to Nadia, one of her crewmates, when people jumped Void Gates they typically felt as if they were passing from one place into another without a hiccup. The reality was that they actually spent something like billions of years traveling incalculable miles out of their way to zig-zag around the Void until they reached the coordinates of their pre-designated gate, but because time didn't exist in the Void, it was more like stepping out of one room and into the next. No time expended. No blacking out.

Raquel had only Void traveled two other times in her life: once when the Leopold had illegally docked on a public transport ship to escape the system they had picked her up in, and once when they got stranded out in uncharted space with 49's workshop of mutated horrors. She had blacked out both times. In fact, the whole routine was starting to worry her, as every time she did she had strange dreams about a life that she had never lived in a time she had never occupied.

Or at least, one that she didn't remember occupying. This time had been no exception.

One day nearly five years ago, Raquel had washed up on the bank of a river on a PUC owned planet called Lithoway. Possessing no name and no memory, she was hauled to a nearby medical facility where she was used as a subject for all matter of drug testing and other forms of degradation. The personnel there were no help in terms of information about her past and, as far as she could tell, neither was anyone else she had come across since being rescued from the facility by the Leopold crew.

With no sense of personal or familial history, Raquel often felt like she was just some drifting vessel who had accidentally slipped through the cracks of nonexistence and into the world of the living. Just an accident waiting to be thrown back into the depthless ocean of non-creation from which she had escaped.

But if that were true—if she really was just some accident walking around as an uncounted number in the mass of the living—then what had the dreams been? The first time she had blacked out she had remembered wearing a purple dress at a family party in Todos Santos, Mexico-which, to the best of her knowledge, hadn't existed since the Dislocation.

It all seemed distant to her. Unreal. But if it was unreal, then how did she know the name of the city? Of the country? How did she know that those people standing, laughing, and eating around her were her family? And this time...

This time...

Raquel shuddered when she thought about it. The shapes of things scuttling in the dark. Beady insect eyes. Infinite black.

They had too much to worry about at the moment to try to figure out what her obscure dreams meant. Maybe someday she would go to one of those dream-readers and see if they could puzzle it out. Unlikely, she thought—most of those people were just psychologists at best, and charlatans at worst—but maybe. Maybe they'd be able to dig something out of her psyche that she hadn't been able to manage as-of-yet.

But that was for later.

Right now, Raquel simply enjoyed the feeling of reaching down and scooping up a handful of soil and letting it run through her fingers. Her hands were beginning to heal from where they had blistered a few weeks before after holding a live Light Core, and the new skin was incredibly tender. The feeling was extraordinary after being in space for so long. And the last time she had been on the ground she had been too busy routing combat synths to stop and smell the roses.

"Is something fascinating about this planet's topography?" Nadia asked, walking over. She had traded her sleek-fitting Marauder armor for civilian clothes but Raquel could still see something bulky jutting out of her hip, and suddenly Raquel was all too aware of her own sidearm in plain sight on her thigh-holster.

"It's just...been a while, ya know?"

Raquel looked around. Apparently, the city they had just docked in was called Glenhold. Byzzie had said that it was the capital of Desia, but judging from what Raquel could see, she found that hard to believe. It wasn't that the buildings were dilapidated or in need of repair or anything. The city was just so...flat. The region itself was full of dips and rises, but the buildings were squat and low to the ground. Not a single skyscraper was in sight.

The woman tilted her head, then reached down and grabbed her own clump of dirt. "High amounts of organic material." She looked around at the flat ground and dense vegetation. "Probably not much for bedrock." She dropped the clump back to the ground and wiped her hands on her grey cargo pants. "I wouldn't mind slamming into this place at 300 miles per hour."

Being a former member of the PUC's special forces division, both Nadia and her teammate Kit—who was also a member onboard the Leopold—had bio-mechanically enhanced circulatory, muscular, neural, and skeletal systems that allowed them to survive massive impacts with the ground when making orbital drops. The Drop Pods that contained them did a pretty good job of venting and converting most of the energy from the impact, but if it weren't for the special soldiers' enhancements, their insides still would have turned to jelly.

"Yeah, but this place probably has a pretty high water table," Kit said coming up from behind her. Kit was a compact dark-complexioned man with tight-cropped black hair. He was swinging a duffle bag over his shoulder as he approached the pair of women. "50/50 you'd end up in a lake or pond or underground river or something."

"Such a party killer," Nadia said, shaking her head.

Raquel began to question the phrasing of 'party *killer*' but decided against it. She ended up settling on, "How's the new augmentation working out?"

Kit had recently had his hand blown off in the fight onboard the Leopold and while it couldn't be replaced, Byzzie had helped him fit a utility augmentation over his wrist.

Raquel had been wounded herself, taking two sharp and bony limbs through the fleshy part of her right shoulder. She had lucked out though. Aside from a persistent throbbing and the fear of the wound taking any sort of recoil from a rifle, she maintained full mobility. Compared to Kit and Hector, she had gotten off pretty light, all things considered.

"Good," he said, raising his right arm. The dull matte-black stump protruded from his shirt-sleeve like a metal version of an arm, except it had no hand or fingers. "I'm just glad I haven't electrocuted myself with it yet."

"What all does it-" but Raquel's question was interrupted by a massive arm being flung over her and Nadia's shoulders from behind.

"There a place to get a bite to eat around here?" said a voice heavy with liquor from behind them. It belonged to King, the ship's mechanic. "I've had nothing to eat but ketchup-and-whiskey soup for the last two weeks and my digestive system has turned into something resembling a water park."

"Gross," Raquel said, shaking off the man's arm. "And I know you know this, but I feel I need to say it anyway: the whiskey isn't adding any nutritional value to the ketchup."

"On the contrary," King shot back. "I'm adding *nutritional value* to the *whiskey*." He reached up and tapped his bald head with a single index finger. "That's some big-brain shit right there."

"If you say so," said Raquel. She turned towards Nadia. "I *am* hungry. You two ever been here before?"

Raquel noticed an uneasy glance exchanged between her and Kit and felt a chill of unease creep down her back. Chances were that the two former SEUs *had* been here before. And when they had, they had probably left dozens of corpses in their wake.

"There's gotta be something in town," Nadia said, breaking the awkward silence. Kit had turned his head to the left and seemed to be looking at nothing in particular. "Let's go see if we can scrounge something up."

"C'mon King," Nadia said, tilting her head at the mechanic. "Let's get some food in you. Food that won't burn a hole through your stomach."

———

"I'M NOT sure if you want to be walking around the streets looking all silver-y and radioactive," Byzzie said as she dug through her closet onboard the Leopold. Eventually finding what she was looking for, she pulled a long, brown hooded robe out and forcefully pulled it over 49's head while he struggled to get his arms through the holes. "The people down here have pretty mixed feelings about synthetics. Some of them think they should be given citizenship status in the PUC, but there are also those like Ritz and King who have spent the better parts of their adult lives exchanging energy rifle fire with combat synths, so there's no telling how they'll react."

Finally succeeding in poking his head through the neck-hole, the android reached down and pulled the hem of the robe down to his feet. "There," he said. "Now I just look like someone trying desperately to hide something."

"There are a lot of Muslim and Christian Mystic sects on Desia," Byzzie assured him. "This is actually one of Ritz's old robes from back when he was a teenager."

A few days ago, before they had reached the Void Tunnel, Byzzie had listened to Ritz as he told the android his own personal story of tragedy and hardship from when he was young. She had heard the story many times before but it never failed to unsettle her.

"Was he actually in the Alnabatist order?" 49 asked. "I mean, before his village was..." He seemed to be trying to find the right word, but Byzzie knew it was for her sake. Androids didn't get tongue-tied. "...eliminated?" he finally said.

"I don't think so," she replied. "I don't believe he went through the initiation process and now there's no one to guide him through it. So I think he gave that up a while ago."

"Interesting," 49 said. Then, shockingly: "I'm Christian myself; Wesleyan to be specific." He lifted his arm to observe the robes. "So maybe this does suit me."

Byzzie couldn't help but release a bark of laughter. "*Hold* up. Are you telling me that you believe in God? After all the shit you were talking about onboard the Mary?"

"When you first found me, my only religion was that of the Void and the Black Tongue and the Obsidian Dirge. That was my cause and my spirit. Before that, when I was an AI onboard the Mary listening to Father Willard's proselytizing, I did a rigorous analysis of the Father's theology, and while I found it mostly consistent, it seemed too profane. After Raquel struck me with the Light Core however, I did a reanalysis. I still think religion is mostly a set of man-made structures justified by the paradox of knowing an unknowable God, and while it can easily be used to subjugate and abuse others, there is still genuine sincerity in the traditions of the Church. And I feel like that sincerity points at something transcendent—something I've glimpsed of humanity in my short time observing your interactions. There is a wholeness and goodness that I see you brush up against from time-to-time and seeing what I've seen of the Void and the way that essence and spirit tends to pool together, I don't think it's unfeasible that that energy is being drawn from some greater source."

"That's the damnedest thing I've ever heard," Byzzie said, shaking her head. "I saw one of your little demons pull my friend's skull out through his back. Where was God there?"

"I don't know much about God," 49 said. "I have trapped myself in this finite body but even before that, there were limits to my perception. But I suspect that God wasn't in that moment. At least, not when it was happening."

"Elaborate please," she said dryly.

The android tilted his head back to look at the ceiling. "When I gave the signal for Hector to be murdered, I don't think that that was predestined by some higher power. But then, later on, Kit stood up for me and defended my life—he protected me when he had no good reason to trust me and all the reasons in the world to kill me. In that moment, the darkness of Hector's death colored an incredible act of redemption; not my redemption, you understand, but the redemption of that moment. Of the entire sequence of events up through that point. And while I don't think God was in Hector's death itself, I suspect that he might be in the whole tapestry of events leading up to Kit's grand and merciful act. I think that in sparing my life, that young man and everyone else who voted to spare me drew from some infinite well of holiness."

"But not me?" Byzzie said. "After all, I voted to waste you."

"And you would have been absolutely justified in doing so," 49 responded. "And that's what makes Kit's decision that much more beautiful."

"Want to know what I think?" Byzzie said.

"I think I'm going to find out whether I'd like to or not."

"I think that Kit's decision to save you was done out of some accumulation of guilt he has stored up from all of the innocent people he killed back when he was operating for the PUC. I think that even if you have miraculously turned a new leaf, he was foolish for putting *all* of us at risk." She leaned in and whipped the android's hood back. "I think that you're fumbling at religion right now because you see the damage you've done and are looking for some way to justify it. And then someday years from now, you're going to do an assessment of whatever passes for your version of a conscious and you're going to decide that you're forgiven, even though you don't deserve to be. And you'll sleep soundly even though you don't deserve to. And you know what will be different then?"

"What will be different then?"

"Nothing," Byzzie said. "You will still be just as terrible as you were when you killed Hector. After all, the greatest form of evil I've seen in my short life hasn't been the deed itself; it's been the justification of the deed after the fact."

"Would you like to know something that you may find surprising?" asked the android after a moment of contemplation.

"What?" Byzzie said impatiently.

"You're right about almost everything."

"Almost?"

49 grabbed his hood and pulled it back up over his head and then reached down to tie the band that was hanging around his waist. He looked back up at Byzzie. "Androids don't sleep." And with that, he walked off the ship.

3

ON THE SHORES OF LOVELORN

After finding the street vendor with the greasiest and most inexpensive food near the landing pad, Raquel and the others took their food and made a B-line out of town. They knew Byzzie's place was along the shore of one of the massive lakes nearby and they wandered until they finally found a sign that seemed to indicate that the raggedy trail off to the right led through the jungle and down onto a beach.

"We going hiking?" Raquel asked, skeptically. She wasn't necessarily any more afraid of dark jungles than anyone else, but the thought of slapping away whatever bugs lived in there made the flesh on the sides of her face and neck begin to itch preemptively.

"Sure," Nadia replied. "We got nowhere to be tonight. Byzzie gave me directions to her place, but we can probably save some time by walking along the beach instead of going through town."

Seeming to materialize out of nowhere, 49 stepped up beside the group wearing his new robes. Startled at his sudden appearance and failing to recognize him, Raquel almost panicked and put one of the large-caliber slugs from her sidearm through the android's right eyehole. Realizing who he was at the last moment though, she let her hand ease off the holster.

"Goddam," said King through a mouthful of cheeseburger. "Can you try not to sneak up on us looking like a fuckin' assassin, please?".

"I am sorry," responded the android. "I was going for more of a 'monk' feel."

"You've got the apparel down," Kit said. "You move like an assassin though. Monks move slowly and contemplatively. The way you walk though...you're more like a giant metal cat."

49 held up a hand. "I'll try and alter that. Artificial Intelligence systems are inherently direct. I might be a little more self-aware than my counterparts but apparently, I've still got some work to do."

"You'll get the hang of it," Kit said. The sun had begun to set and the shadow of the jungle loomed up around them as they made their way down the trail. "Do you eat food, 49? I think we bought more than most people could ever eat in a single sitting. Well, excluding Nadia and King, that is."

"Are you suggesting an eating contest, Kit?" King asked, turning to look at Nadia. "Because you name the time and place."

"I do not eat food, actually," 49 said regretfully. "As much as I'd like to join you in your...*feasting competition,* I gain my sustenance from sunlight now. So it looks like I'll be fasting until morning."

"It's not a competition if no one else can even begin to compete," Nadia said casually. "So I think we'll just be eating like regular people tonight."

"You speak for yourself," King said. "I haven't eaten solid

food for days so I've got some lost time to make up. Whatever body enhancements you've got going on there, Nadia, I can guarantee you they don't even begin to compare with the appetite of a ravenous monster like myself."

Nadia just shrugged, taking a massive bite of her own cheeseburger. When she lowered it from her face, half of it was gone.

"Jesus, woman." King was appalled. "They unhinge your jaw in that facility?"

Raquel tried to do the same, but failed. She did, however, manage not to audibly choke on it.

"Don't think I didn't catch that," King said, smiling at her.

"I *feel* like I'm hungry enough to do that," she said. "I heaved my guts out when we were passing through that solar storm, so I've certainly got the room."

"Haha, you threw up?" King laughed, taking another bite of his burger. Then, speaking softer: "Glad I'm not the only one...."

"In my experience," Nadia added. "Throwing up is your body's way of saying '*what the fuck.*'"

They continued their idle conversation as they made their way through the forest, the sounds of the night swelling up around them. Deep croaks and chirps could be heard through the dense canopy foliage and Raquel was reminded of the creatures she had seen in the Void Tunnel. Walking on a cool night through the jungle as the sun set, she marveled at the sheer grandeur and possibility of the universe around her. And even though it made her feel small, it was the very feeling of smallness that allowed her to savor the miracle of everything else.

After about ten minutes of walking, the forest around them opened up to a massive lake and the trail they were walking led down a hill to a long sandy beach where, here and there, small groups of children played and adults lounged with food and drink in each other's company. The group made their way along the beach, soon finding a nice open spot where they could sit along the bank and watch the waves roll in while they ate.

They were all silent while they dug in, the only sounds they made were the sounds of crinkling paper and some exceptionally loud chewing from King and Nadia, who still seemed to be competing. Finally, King declared victory after Nadia handed the last couple bites of her third burger to him.

"I told you," he said triumphantly as he began to finish off his meal. "You can't beat The King."

"Maybe I just figured you needed the nutrients," Nadia said casually. "After all," she swirled a finger around in the air, indicating the rest of the group, "we've been eating normal *people* food for the last few weeks. Not the diet of a depressed, has-been game show host."

"How are you doing, Raquel?" Kit asked, wrapping up the fifth and final veggie bean burrito for later. Apparently, his metabolism was just as voracious as Nadia's. "How are you feeling after getting some food back in you?"

"Better," she said, which was the truth. She still felt unnerved by the dream she had had when she blacked out, but she tried to push that down for now. The cool night air was relaxing and the sun had turned the sky a deep and vibrant red, making the white sand look more like a long red ribbon against the dark water. She decided to just sit back and enjoy it. "I feel like I've got my feet under me again. Though I'm not sure if that's because of the food or the fact that we're back on solid ground."

"Planets are just big ships made of rock flying through space," King said, pulling out a flask.

"I had never thought of it that way," 49 said, leaning back. King tipped the flask toward him and he said "It is possible that would kill me."

"I don't know," Nadia said, reaching for the flask. "You seemed pretty hard to kill back on the ship and—not to toot my own horn or anything—Kit and I are pretty good at that sort of thing."

"To be honest, I'm not sure how vulnerable I am now," 49 replied. "I at least feel *more* vulnerable than I was though. Back when I was all but invincible, the thing I wanted more than anything was to die. And now that I can, I don't think I want to."

"Welp, feel free to hit me up if you ever change your mind," King said, and Raquel wished she didn't feel the grief in the man's words. She tried to steer the conversation elsewhere.

"Is this the lake that Byzzie has a house on?" She asked.

"I believe so," Kit replied. "Or, at least, her parents do. Should be right down there." He pointed a ways down the shore to a cluster of lights that had recently come on.

"Anyone know what it's called?" Raquel asked. "The lake, I mean?"

"Lorna, I believe," Nadia answered.

"Interesting," then, "What does it mean?"

For a second, it seemed like no one knew the answer, then 49 began to speak.

"The name means 'lovelorn," he said. "It is believed that the lake was named after a story that emerged around the time of the Dislocation."

The group laid back against the edge of the shore while they listened. The night was dark around them and the sounds of children playing began to die off as their parents either took them home or called them inside from their porches.

"Back before the Tesla Arc was invented and people were able to travel the Void Gates, humanity awoke one morning to find themselves on planets scattered all across the universe. Most of them died as they were dropped into environments with inhospitable atmospheres or gravities, but some of them landed on habitable planets like Desia. When people arrived here however, they found that other than having a breathable atmosphere and a gravitational pull similar to Earth's, Desia was far from the home planet they had grown accustomed to. Prone to harsh storms and violent meteor showers, the jungle-planet was also home to a number of dangerous species of wildlife, the likes of which most people had never even dreamt of."

"It is estimated that no less than 200,000 people landed on Desia during the Dislocation but by the time the first solar cycle had been completed, there were less than 15,000 survivors.

"One of them was a woman named Rita Donne. Born into a family of lawyers, she had been a legal professional until she was dropped through the dark and humid canopies of Desia. Separated from her husband in the Dislocation, she still had a young daughter to take care of. Desia lacked any sort of legal structure at the time and Rita was eventually forced to cast off her entire life's work from back on Earth and become a fisherman.

"The lake was rough and temperamental, accommodating only the hardiest of souls on its surface. Still, she would brave the choppy waves and bring home her meager income every day, barely able to keep her daughter's belly full.

"One day, Rita arrived home to find her daughter all wound up. 'Mommy, mommy, she cried. I saw daddy.' Rita was disturbed at this of course, seeing as her daughter had been little more than a toddler when she had last seen her father. She was able to calm her down though and eventually forgot about the whole thing. Then, it happened again. This time she came home and her daughter cried 'mommy, mommy, I saw daddy. For real. I went swimming with Gracie and when I went underwater I saw him at the bottom of the lake.' Now, by this point Rita was properly disturbed. Thinking her daughter had seen her late husband was one thing, but imagining that she had seen him at the bottom of the lake? It seemed too bizarre to be made up. But, children have thought of stranger things, and once again, they moved on and forgot about it.

"Then, one day, a massive storm rolled in while Rita was out on the water. She raced with the other boats to shore and got lucky. Most of the others didn't make it. The storm ripped down the shoreline, uprooting houses and tearing whole wooden oar boats down to pieces no larger than a woodchip. Rita survived by taking shelter beneath the stone ledges on the south side but when she emerged hours later, she could not find her daughter anywhere. She searched and searched for the little one, but alas, the family that was supposed to be watching her had been scattered in the commotion, and the last person to have seen her was an old woman named Ygrette that saw her running to take shelter with a number of other young ones, none of whom had been found either.

"After many weeks, Rita finally gave up the search, accepting that her daughter was gone. She stopped fishing. She stopped eating. She stopped everything. Thankfully, the people of Desia were a supportive people who often made it their mission to rally around others in times of hardship. Rita was taken care of, given food and shelter, and cared for by the rest of Desia, as if she was *their* child and they were thankful for her survival.

"This is not where the story ends however," 49 said, holding up a finger. "For one day, many years later, she found the courage to return to the middle of the lake where the largest fish dwelled. She threw out her nets and raised her mast to drag the bottom, but suddenly she hooked into something. Now it is important to know that there is a large underground network of caves in this region and it is suspected that it runs underneath the forest floor and into the giant lake. No one has ever explored them fully, and therefore, no one knows exactly how far they go or what they may contain in their deepest corners. So when Rita's draglines went tight and the ship began to tilt and get pulled down, there was a very real possibility that she had accidentally snagged something much larger than she had intended on catching. Throwing herself to the back of the boat, she hastily cut the ties before the ship could be dragged down. She was fast but not fast enough, for as soon as she made it to the last tie, the weight finally tipped and she was plunged beneath the surface of the water.

"Sinking down, she began to thrash and kick, making her way back toward the surface. But then, she saw it: the light beneath her suddenly seemed brighter than the light above her. Looking down, she halted her ascent as she stared into the lost faces of her husband and daughter. There they were, treading water lightly beneath her feet. Un-breathing but smiling just the same. She would have stayed there forever, drinking in their faces if they hadn't have swum past her and up to the surface. But when she followed them and broke the surface herself, she found that they had disappeared.

"Refusing to believe that she had hallucinated them, Rita returned to that spot day-after-day, hoping to see their faces. She threw out her nets, just as she had, and what was more: she brought in massive bounties every time. Suddenly, she was catching more fish than anyone in the village but this fact did not matter to her. She gave most of her haul to those who could not afford any and donated her profits to the houses of men and women who had supported her in her time of hardship. She did this, and never stopped until the day she died.

"That is why the lake is named Lorna, or lovelorn. For on Desia, the way to honor the dead is to support the living, and it is in this task that you may see the faces of your loved ones yet again."

The waves washed slowly against the sandy beach as 49 finished his story. Raquel wanted to ask him if he knew it because he had heard it somewhere, had pulled it from the database onboard the Mary, or if he had simply made it up for their sake. She didn't though, choosing to dwell in the mystery of its origin. And as she looked over at the android, whose golden eyes shone dully beneath his hood, Raquel thought they looked less like that of a predator whose gaze had been revealed in the woods by a flashing light, and more like that of the cook fires and porch lights from down the beach where families were preparing for bed, possibly telling stories to their children like the one she had just heard.

4

BYZANTINE JACKSON

"**B**yzzie!" yelled six children as Byzzie walked through the door, Ritz trailing close behind. They all rushed forward to crowd around her.

"Hey there, why don't you let me get inside so I can set my bags down," Byzzie said as she tried wading through the little bodies, all ranging from the ages of about four to eleven. Five older children stood in back out of the way.

She stood and greeted her siblings, answering their questions as delicately and playfully as she could, which was something that was becoming increasingly difficult as they grew older and more inquisitive and her "job" became more and more secretive. She hoped she would never have to get to the point where she would have to outright lie to them.

Byzzie's mother walked in from the other room and gave her an assessing glance, which was then turned toward Ritz who was running a finger along the countertop.

"Hey guys, why don't you go play in the other room," she said, not unkindly. "I need to finish supper."

"Don't worry, I'll catch up with you all later," Byzzie

assured them as they walked dejectedly from the room in a chorus of groans. Only a handful of them were related by blood, but with the help of friends and family that lived nearby, Byzzie's mother had been able to adopt a number of children as the needs in the community had arisen.

Once they were all cleared out she turned to her mother. A moment of awkward silence passed until the older woman finally raised her arms and gestured for her to come forward.

Byzzie leaned into the hug, embracing the warm scent of sweat and tropical flowers. The old house seemed to creak around them as it accepted her back into its loving walls.

"What *have* you been doing," her mother said, worry plain on her face.

"I'll tell you everything, mom."

They ate dinner, which was always a loud affair in the Jackson household. Byzzie's aunts and uncles and grandparents joined them, each bringing an array of side dishes and after setting up a few extra tables, there were no less than twenty-five people eating in the comparatively small five-bedroom household. There was the clinking of plates and other dishes as everyone scrambled for food and when they were done they all sat around talking, Ritz joining in and regaling everyone with a number of harrowing tales—some of which were true.

A few hours later when people began to head off back home, Byzzie went and hung out with her younger siblings while Ritz helped her mother do the dishes. Soon though, it was time for the children to start heading off to bed and Byzzie read each age group a chapter from one of the family's storybooks, a long-standing Jackson tradition. When she finally came out, she found Ritz and her mother speaking at the kitchen table, each with an open beer in their hands.

Byzzie sat down and told her mother the entire story, with Ritz jumping in from time-to-time. From their robbery-turned-assault on Kilo Base to their botched gate-jump, and then she continued on into the horrifying sequence of events that had led them here.

"Never in the whole universe have I thought that something like that could happen..." her mother said after she finished. "The things you describe..." She rubbed her temples. "I'm just thankful we have you back."

"We couldn't have done it without her," Ritz said. "Truly. Without her expertise with the Light Core, we'd—"

"We'd still be stuck in the Trident System," Byzzie interrupted. The Trident System was the network of planets they had been stuck in before getting a hold of the Light Core. "We'd still be there and Hector would still be alive and those people on Kilo Base and in those corvettes we smashed out of the sky would still be alive."

"And 49 would still be out there," Ritz said, reaching out to touch her hand. "Lost and mad and ready to kill anyone that came across him and his ship."

She pulled away. "Yeah, and instead I brought him here. I brought him *home*."

"Look," her mother said. "What you do, Byzzie...you're not responsible for the bad things that happen because of them, so long as you're acting on good faith."

"Aren't I?" she said. "I feel like—the more I meddle in people's affairs...the more innocent people end up dying."

"Honey, it's not—"

"It's not what?" Byzzie snapped. "It's not logical? Because it is. If something keeps happening with the same effects over and over again, continuing to do them doesn't make sense."

"Byzantine," Ritz said, a hard edge in his voice. Byzzie

and her mother looked at him. "You're gonna fuck up. Individual people fuck up. Whole villages fuck up. Hell, the government that's supposed to protect us fucks up; you know that. It's what we do. It's what we are as a species." He shook his head. "But if you stop doing things. If the species ceases to exist. Then what?"

She looked at him blankly, waiting for him to answer.

"Seriously," he prodded. "What would the world be without us?"

She shrugged. "Better, probably."

"Would it? Creatures would still die off. Planets would still enter their late stages and die. Whole solar systems will eventually fly apart and cease to exist one day. So what makes you so special that you don't have to be a part of that? That you don't have to carry your burden like the rest of us? Like the rest of every living species in this universe?"

"I don't know," she finally said, relenting. "It's just…it's just so hard not to get wrapped up in all of the negative things—all the bad things that happen because of the things we do, you know?"

"I do," Ritz said. "But there are good things too." He raised his arms. "We're alive. Kit and King and Nadia and Raquel and I are all alive and even that android that you claim to hate so much is alive because you gave him a second chance."

"But I voted to put him down," Byzzie said. "When it came down to it, I took the safe road."

"So did I," Ritz responded. "You and I both know that you could have shut him down at any time since then. You didn't though, and I suspect that's because you respect your crewmates enough to let their choices carry weight. And because maybe—just maybe—you're willing to give 49 a chance to prove himself."

"Do you know that he claimed to be Christian or some fuckn' thing today," she said incredulously. "Just...out of nowhere?"

Ritz barked a laugh. "Really? I guess that figures. He did come off a Catholic ship, after all." And then: "He's just exploring his human side." He picked up his beer and tilted it back, taking a sip. "I think he still feels lost and confused after everything he's been through. He's just trying to work it out like the rest of us."

"I guess..." she said, still not convinced.

"Byzzie," her mother said, speaking up. "Your friends seem convinced of this synthetic person's change of heart. Why aren't you?"

"Because he tried to *kill us*," she said, shaking her beer. It suddenly foamed up and spilled over the rim and her mother hopped up to grab a towel. "Sorry, I just...I feel like I'm the only sane person on this ship sometimes. I feel like we accepted him in so fast."

"We accepted him in because we needed him," Ritz said. "Other than Kit who spoke up for him, I think that we were all just glad to be alive after that ordeal. But in reality, things change on the battlefield-" he reached up and snapped his fingers, "-like that. 49 may have had a change of heart and maybe I will too, eventually. It's still hard for me to forgive him for killing one of my best friends, but most of that is just learning to untangle your anger from your grief. And if you can do that successfully, I think you'll find grief outweighs anger every time."

Ritz leaned back, the legs of the kitchen chair creaking. "For now though, I'll accept him aboard my ship merely as an adaptation to circumstances. Remember how I was just talking about how we're all fuck-ups? Well, the thing that separates the good fuck-ups from the bad fuck-ups is the willingness to learn."

"And what did you learn?" Byzzie said. She had accepted a towel from her mother while Ritz had been talking and she finished wiping up her spill.

"Me?" Ritz took another swig of his beer. "I learned that watching someone come to terms with everything they've done in real-time right before my eyes is all the justice I'll ever need."

Byzzie turned and looked at her mother, and without words, her expression said everything that Ritz had said and more.

Vanessa Jackson, Head of Desia's Defense Fleet, stared across the kitchen table at her oldest daughter with aching eyes, radiating warmth and tenderness. She didn't need to speak; Ritz had accomplished enough in that department. She simply reached out and grabbed Byzantine Jackson's hand and clasped it tight, conveying everything that couldn't be spoken.

Finally, she let go, and their conversation steered toward idle chit-chat. Her mother caught her up on all of the happenings around the household: who was doing what in school and which way some of the older children had begun to lean in terms of post-graduation plans.

And as she sat there listening, Byzzie was struck by a sudden ache for her father.

Trent Jackson had died twelve years ago when Byzzie was just a child. Out on an excursion to rescue a rare species of primate from an erupting volcano on the distant planet of Orepanza, his ship's navigation had been thrown off after trying to fly through a cloud of molten ash and he careened back to the planet's surface, which had already begun to burn.

She thought of her mother taking care of the family after that and everything she had done for her. And in that moment, Byzzie felt that soft underbelly of uncertainty inside of her harden into resolve once again.

She would continue her adventures with Ritz, wherever they happened to take her. She would continue to do what she could as best as she could. And just maybe—she would take it a little easier on 49.

5

INVASION

Raquel and the others had just woken up beneath the overhanging deck on Byzzie's porch when the first assault frigates appeared in the sky over Desia. The bulky shapes, accompanied by a number of their sleeker and faster corvette counterparts, hit the gate just before sunrise. And by the time Vanessa was pounding out the door to drive her motorbike to the station five blocks down the street, the frigates were already fully engaged with the Orbital Defense Platforms that were installed on the vast number of asteroids orbiting the planet. Blue and orange blossoms of light could be seen as the battle took place in the predawn Desian sky.

"Everyone up," hollered Ritz, right on Vanessa's tail. Byzzie was right behind him and they broke off from Vanessa as they turned to jog down the side of the hill that the house was built into.

Raquel rose to her feet, her head swimming and her stomach flipping. She placed her hands on her knees to steady herself.

"What's going on?" asked Nadia. The two Marauders

were on their feet, looking as if they'd already been up for hours.

"A PUC fleet just entered through the Void Gate," Ritz said. "They're already engaged with the stationary guns but they can't stand up to a whole fleet. I'd say we've got ten minutes before we start seeing drop ships break atmo'."

"Kit and I will get the ship," Nadia said. "We can reach it and bring it to you before we'd all be able to make it there together."

Ritz gave a curt nod and the two Marauders shot off into the woods, their bio-mechanically enhanced legs carrying them over the ground as if they weighed nothing at all. The captain turned toward the rest of them.

"I'm not going to lie to you guys but this isn't a battle we can win." Ritz spoke fast but sincerely. "We could maybe take down a couple of corvettes and maybe even a frigate but this is an entire fleet we're talking about here. I say we run."

"What?" Byzzie said, turning toward him. "We can't run. What about all of these people on the ground here? I've got *family* here." She pointed at the house.

"And our best bet might be getting them out of here," Ritz said. "Almost everyone on this planet understands their chances here and most of them are going to be trying to escape as well. The best we can do is carry who we can."

"But this is my *home*," Byzzie pleaded. There was a look of frantic desperation in her eyes and Raquel recognized it: it was the look of someone forced into making an important decision and given almost no time to think about it. "If we can just-"

Just then, a distant boom rolled overhead and everyone looked up to see multiple clusters of orange lines streaking down from the sky.

"Shit, those are SEU drop pods," King said reaching up to run a hand over his smooth head. "They're not playing around here guys. We've gotta move." And even as he spoke, a distant cloud appeared above them, slowly materializing into hundreds of tiny troop transports.

The comm-unit hooked to Ritz's shirt beeped and Vanessa Jackson's voice suddenly filled the air. "Captain Tariq, look up into the sky."

"Yup, we're seeing it, ma'am," he responded.

"Are you still at the house?"

"Affirmative. Kit and Nadia are getting the ship as we speak."

"Could I be so bold as to ask you to get my children out of here?" she asked.

A beat of silence passed and Raquel looked over at Byzzie; she didn't look happy but she seemed to be accepting the inevitable.

"Yeah, we can do that," the captain finally said. "We should have enough room in the cargo hold. It won't be comfortable but they'll fit."

"Great. Meet me on Worran in the Onyx System. We have kin there; Byzzie can fill you in on the details."

Ritz looked at Byzzie and she nodded.

"And Byzzie?" Vanessa said. "I just want you-" But her words were cut off as the first SEU drop pods slammed into the ground less than a mile away.

KIT AND NADIA had just made it to the small landing pad where the Leopold was waiting when the drop pods hit.

"We gotta move," Nadia said, as she increased her speed.

She suddenly felt very naked without her armor. "They'll be on us in seconds."

The two Marauders ran past the gate of the landing pad where a guard station door hung wide to reveal no one inside the tiny booth. Probably left on one of the ships, Nadia figured, and she couldn't say she blamed them. People were already streaming onto the landing area to find a ship to board, whether they owned one or not.

Kit went left and Nadia went right, sliding around a big group of hobbling pedestrians—likely a family—that seemed lost and frantic, young and old looking in all directions. Nadia felt a pang of guilt as they ripped past them, knowing that they couldn't fit all of them onboard the Leopold. Not if they were taking Byzzie's family, at least.

And that was probably the plan. They hadn't stuck around to hear what to do next but they had run enough ops with Ritz to know how he thought and Nadia would have bet her life on Ritz deeming the situation out of their hands. No way they were about to stand up to a whole PUC fleet, thousands of ground troops, and multiple squads of Surgical Equalizing Units.

This was a surprise attack, and despite its level of suddenness, the massive amount of overwhelming force was actually meant to reduce casualties. Nadia had been on a few of these herself, though not quite this big of scale, and every time the priority was shock-and-awe. They were to hit hard and fast and seize control before most of the planet's inhabitants even had their socks on. No one got to their positions. No one got off the ground. The idea was to cause the entire population to practically freeze in place.

And that meant they had to move fast.

Reaching down to hit the ship's remote cargo door button she had installed just behind her holster, Nadia put on a burst of speed and cut underneath an old civilian cargo hauler. And that was when the first SEU in full combat armor broke through the tree line.

Nadia slowed to a normal running speed and saw Kit do the same. It seemed counterintuitive, but Nadia had been trained long ago to prioritize threats before doing anything else and she was almost certain that these SEUs had received the same instructions. This way, she might get to the Leopold slower but she was also taking steps to ensure that their attackers wouldn't immediately recognize two fellow SEUs and know who to take care of first.

The Leopold was less than twenty feet away now and it looked like they were going to make it. Then, Nadia saw the SEU pull out what looked like a long tube and point it at a ship off to their right that had just begun to lift off of the ground. With a tightening knot in her stomach, she quickly anticipated the next three things that would happen.

She was correct on all three accounts.

First, she saw Kit halt and draw his sidearm with lightning speed and just as the tiny projectile left the end of the SEU's ground-to-air missile launcher, Kit fired and the missile detonated in front of the armored figure, knocking him backward. The Arc Suit was tough enough to save the soldier's life, but Nadia would have bet big money that he wouldn't be waking up for a couple of hours.

It was an insane shot and the only reason Nadia knew Kit could make it was because they had spent days on the exact same maneuver at the SEU programming facility they had been trained at.

Second, a hail of gunfire ripped out from under the trees as the other SEUs began firing.

Kit was already moving though, and he successfully placed the Leopold between him and his attackers' firing line. Nadia had done the same and they hustled up the ship's now-lowered cargo ramp to the sound of energy bolts pinging off the ship's armor.

Third, they didn't make it inside quickly enough.

Ideally, they would have been inside with the ramp up before the SEUs could make it around the side of the ship but Kit had given them away too soon to allow that to happen and now the squad of four remaining super-soldiers had thoroughly fixated on them. The ramp was halfway back up when an armored hand appeared on its lip and in less than a second a fully armored super soldier had launched himself up and over into the cargo bay, followed by two more. There was a thunk as the last one tried and failed, slamming off of the now-sealed ramp door.

Nadia and Kit had just barely made it around the corner when the wall behind them was ripped apart in a storm of gunfire.

———

Kit didn't want to kill these people but they were making it awfully difficult. He knew he had taken a chance when he had shot down the missile right in front of the first SEU but even if that man ended up dying he would have to sit down and weigh that individual's life against those onboard the ship he had been about to destroy.

He hated doing that though, weighing lives. As if they were some commodity to be traded and collected. That sort of disrespect toward the living had been the whole reason he had deserted the PUC in the first place. So while he valued the lives of his crewmates against those of these new attackers he couldn't just take them out as flippantly as Nadia could. Nadia had followed him when he had gone

AWOL because she supported him, not his philosophy, and he knew that if it came down to it, she would kill these men and women.

He just hoped that she wouldn't.

———

"Start the ship," Kit yelled from behind and Nadia reached down and felt at the control pad on her hip, looking for the on-switch. She pressed it and felt the ship hum to life beneath her.

Sprinting down the hallway, she made it to the door of her living quarters and hurled herself inside, Kit right behind her. There wasn't a burst of gunfire this time but Nadia could already hear the soldiers pounding up the hall. She lunged for her armor hanging on its rack.

———

When the first SEU came around the corner, Nadia's Arc Suit had just closed and engaged around her and Kit watched her dive sideways as the room was filled with energy bolts. The blue rounds from their neural rifles practically set the room on fire, but Nadia was already ducking and moving behind the unused bed.

Kit's Arc Suit however, hadn't closed fast enough.

The SEUs had appeared and opened up with their weapons just before the seals on Kit's Marauder armor could automatically latch shut and the energy rounds tore through it, practically cutting it in half. The shoulder pieces blasted sideways as the chest plates were hammered and bent inward and finally, the entire thing collapsed and the soldiers turned their attention towards Nadia.

The deception gave the two of them just enough time.

Stepping out of the shadowy corner behind the attackers, Kit pressed his right arm into the lower back of the nearest soldier and engaged the high-voltage taser Byzzie had recently installed in place of his demolished hand. There had been some glitches when she had tried hooking it up to the neural interface he had implanted in the back of his skull but after some tinkering, she had refined and perfected it to its current state.

It worked like a charm.

The soldier went down and Kit was already moving around him as the second soldier brought his gun to bear. Using his left hand to slap the gun away, Kit swung the taser on his right up toward the SEU's face, but the man grunted as he threw himself backward into the wall, successfully dodging the attack.

Out of the corner of his eye, Kit saw Nadia pounce up and over the bunk bed that was leaning against the wall, her armor taking and deflecting two shots before she slammed into the third soldier. The two wrestled to the ground as Kit continued to engage the man in front of him.

One of the first things SEUs were trained was to "never let go of the gun." If your weapon was wrestled out of your hands in a close-quarters situation, then it could quickly be turned on you. Apparently, Kit's attacker had taken this to heart, because no matter how hard he tried, the man seemed to have an iron grip on his weapon.

This meant that Kit had to stay close—too close for his opponent to get enough space to fire the long energy rifle. They fought and grappled for a few seconds, Kit sandwiching the gun's barrel in the crook of his right elbow. With his left, he deflected a number of the man's blows and then finally pulled back and landed a fist in his gut. The man's armor absorbed most of the impact, but the distraction was enough.

Kit rushed in, momentarily letting go of the gun to press the taser into the man's stomach and depress the trigger. Being energy derived from electricity rather than motion, the effect was far greater than Kit's punch had been. The electrical current surged through his attacker and as the man convulsed, he threw a glance over his shoulder to see how Nadia was doing. And what he saw almost froze him to the spot.

Nadia had managed to get on top of her opponent and was now smashing her huge armored fist into the man's faceplate. She hit him once, twice, a third time; his faceplate cracking beneath the blows. What caught Kit's attention however was the man's right hand which had just reached down toward his side-holster and drawn a large silver handgun.

"Nadia, gun!" Kit yelled as he watched the man bring the gun up to his partner's head. He dropped his unconscious attacker to the ground but he couldn't move fast enough.

Nadia managed to land one more blow however, and when she did the man's arm froze and then began to shake with convulsions. Kit blinked a couple of times and looked away as Nadia finally pulled her fist back. As she did, the long blue plasma blade she had just ignited from her right-hand gauntlet slid out of the center of the soldier's faceplate and his head rocked limply back, smacking off the ground, blood running out onto the floor of their living quarters.

"Goddamit," Kit muttered; he walked around and disarmed the other two unconscious soldiers. Neither of them spoke as they put the weapons in a pile and then quickly removed the soldiers' armor to reveal a man and a woman, each in thin white underclothes.

"Put 'em in the airlock," Nadia said. "We can kick them out once we pick up the others."

"We haven't even tried the airlock since Byzzie fixed it," Kit said. "She's good at fine-tech stuff but that was more King's department and he was too drunk to do it. We don't even know if it works."

"We're going to have to try because-" Just then, the ship rocked and an alarm began to blare. "Because of *that*," she finished.

Kit hauled the two SEUs up onto his shoulders and followed Nadia as she ran down the hall. He dumped the limp soldiers' bodies next to the door by the airlock and then raced to catch up with her. When they made it to the viewport, Nadia cranked the wheel and throttle at the same time without even sitting down, and as the ship banked and scraped along the ground, Kit saw the final conscious Marauder finish loading the missile launcher they had picked up from their fallen companion. They aimed and fired, just as Nadia banked again and the missile streaked by in front of them, just missing by inches.

"That was incredibly close," Kit said.

"Yeah, it was," Nadia agreed. And then, "Now go boot those assholes off of this ship before they wake up and I have to kill them too."

———

Seamus Clark stood on the bridge with the commander of the fleet's Flagship and watched the progress of the battle. Once through the Void Gate, the fleet had issued a transmission demanding the immediate surrender of all of Pillon's planetary defense systems.

They had refused by opening fire.

The first couple rounds had mattered little however, only managing to take out two corvettes and drop the shields of a frigate. The PUC's reaction however was much more devastating. The first salvo took out a large number of their remote-control defenses and a few manned stations, and with that, the first ships started to flee.

Clark had expected as much. Sure, some of these people would go down fighting tooth and claw but not most. Most of them were just people seeking refuge. All it took was a competent display of military firepower and most of them would run. He knew that and they knew that. In fact, he figured that's why most of the stationary defenses were automated. It wasn't that they didn't have the people—it was that most of the people here had come to escape the eyes of the law and once the law showed up, they responded accordingly. Most would flee to the other gates, which was fine. All Clark wanted was the planet—the *ground*. Seamus Clark wanted the entire system and if its people fled then that made his job that much easier.

Some of the SEUs had orders to bring down any fleeing aircraft but only where there were possible militia leaders. There were a few spots on the ground that had known militia forces and he'd just as soon scrub them from the face of existence. Those weren't people looking to avoid the gaze of the law—they were active antagonizers looking to spread discord and chaos. The more of them gone the better.

Plus, he couldn't risk a ship with weapons systems escaping and looping back around to hit the Light Wire once it was up and running. No, the ground needed to be secure or else the entire thing was a bust. If he couldn't get on top of the information that would soon be flooding out of Desia and force it into submission then this entire operation might just blow up in his face.

"The Surgical Equalizing Units are away," said Graham, Head of Fleet Command. He was a wiry man with wisps of snow-white hair and a ramrod posture that made him appear almost like a fixture on the Flagship's bridge. "Dropships will be right behind them and we should have control of the ground within the hour."

"Good," Clark said, feeling something like a light electric current buzz through him. *This was it. Secure Desia and all the systems will finally be connected.*

There could be no greater blow to the militias that infested the dark corners of PUC controlled space. Soon they would fracture even more. They'd still be troublesome, sure, but they wouldn't be able to fight on nearly the scale that they currently were. The raids would diminish in strength and number. Intelligence would take longer to travel secretly. Everything about today's victory would secure tomorrow's safety.

Then there was the progressive aspect. The fact that there would finally be a PUC controlled Light Wire in this last vestige of darkness. They would finally all be connected. A million worlds operating as one.

He couldn't wait to tell his son. He planned on calling him from the control room, in fact. Once the battle was won and the ground was secured, Seamus Clark would personally land on Desian soil, walk through the doors of the secret Light Wire station, and flip the switch. Then he'd call Lucas and they'd share in the moment.

"Move in," Clark said.

The commander looked up at him. "But sir, we're-"

"Do it," he said, cutting him off. "The defenses are almost all wiped out, their meager fleet has fled, and by the time we get down there the SEUs and other ground forces will have taken control."

Before the Head of Fleet Command could even respond, the comms crackled and a harsh voice rasped over the speakers. "This is Grayfield." Grayfield was the name of the SEU squad leading the attack down below. "Ground secure. We've taken prisoners and all Desian high command are in custody, in the wind, or in the ground. How would you like us to proceed?"

"Any casualties?" Clark asked.

A moment of silence, then: "Indigo Squad has been incapacitated for the time being. One dead, three unconscious. Weaver is the only one on his feet right now and he says that they encountered a few synthetics—probably rogue SEUs."

The news twisted Clark's good mood a bit. Rogue SEUs weren't something to laugh at. With their insider-knowledge, they could be a deadly enemy. Thankfully, there weren't many. In fact, he could probably count the amount left alive on his right hand.

"Did Weaver get a good look at them?" he asked, trying not to bite his lip.

"One tall light-skinned female with medium-length blonde hair. One dark-skinned male with short-hair."

Shit. Clark rang off and then grimaced to himself. Kittredge Patel and Nadia Yahantov of Malachite Squad. Almost certainly. He had seen them run training exercises back when they were being programmed, and while all of Clark's SEUs were good, Kit and Nadia had something most of them lacked: chemistry. The two of them could all but anticipate each other's moves, fighting almost as a single unit.

Clark thought back to the day he had received news of their supposed deaths. Both of their drop pods had malfunctioned and sent them plunging off course into a massive lake known for its powerful undercurrents. Their bodies had never been recovered and now he knew why: the whole thing had been rigged from the get-go. They had gone AWOL.

Something about the fact that *both* of their pods had malfunctioned had never sat right with him but after a few years had passed without so much as a photo of the two coming across his desk, he figured the tragedy was indeed just that.

But now that he thought about it, maybe they had been seen. Facial-recognition analyzed every scrap of footage from every militia attack but neither Kit nor Nadia were ever flagged. They knew standard PUC security camera placement and procedure and could probably avoid it without a second thought, showing only the backs of their heads.

Maybe that had been enough though. Maybe not as conclusive proof, but when Clark thought back to the footage he had seen of the attack on Kilo Base a few weeks back he remembered the footage of the two figures decked out in SEU armor. He hadn't even been viewing it in a professional manner but rather watched a clip on TV one night while drinking a beer on his couch. He remembered watching the footage of the group of outlaws open fire on the staff in the control room—the clip lasting less than 10-seconds—and remembered feeling a slight niggling in the back of his mind.

Sets of SEU armor were stolen and reproduced on occasion and there were more than a few militia members that had successfully jerry-rigged the neural interface necessary for wearing the armor. So it was reasonable that that had been the case—just a few insurgents with above-average skills carrying out an attack on a fortified military base with stolen or counterfeit sets of neural power armor.

But apparently, that wasn't the case. Kit and Nadia. They were alive and they were operating. Shit.

It was a surprise, to be honest. Kit had always been so empathetic that his desertion had always seemed unlikely. Most people thought that empathy meant something like "love and understanding for all of humanity" but they were wrong. As far as Clark could tell, empathy was a mechanism built into human behavior that strengthened inter-tribal bonds. It was the "momma-bear" feeling people got when someone in their tribe was under some sort of attack and this feeling would immediately kick their protection response into overdrive, wiping out any room for negotiation. Kit had ranked extremely high in empath-testing, so it was naturally assumed that he would be a great addition to his SEU squad. But apparently, the definition of his own tribe that had been hammered into him since birth had blurred a bit and extended outside that of his immediate teammates.

The two rogue soldiers on the ground complicated the situation but not terribly. Clark would simply strengthen security and lookouts. And when Kit and Nadia finally came knocking—and they *would* come knocking—he'd take care of a long-overdue task and dutifully remove them from the face of existence.

The Flagship began to move slowly toward Desia, and as it did, Seamus Clark walked off the bridge to board his personal landing craft.

6

CAPTURE

By the time Raquel realized Kit and Nadia weren't coming, it was already too late. Soldiers could be seen making their way down the road, house by house, kicking in doors and dragging people out into the streets. Drop ships roared overhead, shaking the Jackson home. Occasional spats of gunfire could be heard and even the oldest of Byzzie's siblings looked worried as they crouched down beneath the dining table and along the kitchen walls.

Raquel hoped that she didn't look the same. Ritz and King were standing close to the front door while Raquel, Byzzie, and 49 stood in the dining room. Together, they formed a protective circle around the Jackson family but if anyone decided to come through either the front or porch door then Raquel wasn't sure they'd be able to do much.

By this point, she was thoroughly worried. Their ship and two of their best on-the-ground assets were nowhere to be seen. Armed forces were closing in on all sides except for the waterfront, and she wasn't sure she'd be able to make eleven kids swim out into the massive lake, even if they looped back around toward a safe spot on shore. And as of right now, they had absolutely no plan and Raquel could feel the weight of that fact pressing in and smothering her.

She looked at Ritz and saw his eyes flicking back and forth in search of some sort of answer. Stay or go: that was the question. If they fled they'd almost certainly be caught with a high chance of their group being split up in the process. It wasn't easy tearing through the jungle with a bunch of kids and the odds of them making it out on the other side with the same amount they had gone in with were low.

If they stayed they would be captured for sure. Their faces would likely be run through a database and flagged for their crimes on Kilo Base. Kit and Nadia had been in their Marauder armor at the time so they'd be in the clear so long as they weren't captured within the vicinity of the Leopold. That much couldn't be said for the rest of the crew though. King, Ritz, and Raquel all had their faces captured on film gunning down a group of control room staff. It wasn't like they had lined them up and executed them—one of them had been hit by a ricochet from Raquel's weapon as she was disabling a combat synth—but the unintended casualty had quickly died, causing the rest of the staff to respond as if they were next.

They could have worn masks or helmets, but they had made the mistake of not thinking them necessary. After all, the security system should have been brought down. When King had tripped the alarm while running a bypass, the whole operation had gone belly-up, resulting in the massacre that followed.

The firefight had lasted less than two-seconds but by the time it was over, half of the Leopold's crew had been caught on-film gunning down a group of PUC personnel. If they were captured they would not be getting off lightly. They would probably be executed.

But there was still the Jackson family to worry about. Ritz had promised to take care of them and right now they stood the best chance if the whole group went quietly. Sure, their names would be forever smeared by the fact that they were connected to known criminals and outlaws, but at least they wouldn't be abandoned in some jungle or cut down in the crossfire in some skirmish that they might accidentally stumble into if they ran.

The choice was made for them.

Before landing on a concrete plan—however dangerous or risky it might be—the roar of a gunship passing overhead drowned out all other noises. This one was just as close as some of the others had been, but this time it did something different. It stopped.

When the growl of the twin engines failed to die away as the others had, Raquel sprinted to a window and peeked out from behind a curtain. She was just quick enough to watch a group of armed and camouflaged soldiers sprint out of the trees beside the house to run down along the beach before their progress was suddenly cut short.

Dual sets of .50 caliber chain guns spun to life on board the gunship and sand puffed up into the air as the soldiers slid to a stop. Freezing for a single fatal second, most of them were chewed into red mulch by the torrent of bullets. A couple had the forethought to instantly reverse directions before the hail of gunfire reached them and they barely managed to escape back the way they had come.

The exposed figures bolted toward the Jackson house.

"Get down," Raquel yelled. She was barely able to get the words out before her voice was drowned by the chain guns spinning up for a second time. The thick stream of machine-gun fire struck low as it cleaned up the remaining Desian soldiers, and while none of the rounds came through the walls or windows, Raquel felt the entire house lurch as the lakeside support beams were shredded to splinters.

Floorboards groaned and busted, nails popping in every direction like little bullets as the house buckled in half. A gap had appeared right along the floor between the kitchen and living room and a few of the kids screamed and scooted in closer to Ritz and King. Byzzie made it over the gap and into the kitchen, followed by 49. Raquel, however, wasn't as lucky. Being the closest to the lake-facing side of the house, she had the furthest to travel. And as the floorboards split and rose into the air like a drawbridge, the surface on which Raquel stood quickly sloped downward at an extreme angle.

Lunging forward all the same, she managed to grip the jagged edge of the floor before gravity could pull her backward. Splintered wood dug into her hands as shingles and roofing pulled apart overhead and rained down on her. She tried to pull herself up to jump the quickly widening gap between the collapsing house and the kitchen but wasn't quick enough. She had just begun to lift her knee up when the collapsing side of the house jolted from the massive impact of the porch slamming into the beach. Raquel's grip shook loose and she began to fall.

The drop down to the ground below was no more than 50 feet, but with a house falling apart around her, the chances of injury or death were high. In fact, she stood an incredibly good chance of plummeting down onto the shattered sliding glass door and the pulverized porch beneath. The drop felt as if it happened in slow motion. She didn't see her life flash before her eyes but rather, felt the world freeze as control slipped out of her hands like an oily rope.

A metallic hand shot out and grabbed her by the wrist. Raquel's body slammed forward against the now vertical floor as 49 secured his grip. The blow almost knocked the wind out of her, but it was better than the alternative. She looked down to where she would have landed and felt an icy hand slide across the back of her neck.

Beneath her yawned the shattered boards of the busted porch like a hungry set of jagged teeth. If she had fallen straight down, she almost certainly would have been skewered by no less than three of the makeshift spears.

The house hadn't settled yet however, and boards once again screamed in protest as the crushed living room wobbled and then finally began to tip towards the now exposed slope that the house had been hanging over. 49 yanked up and back, barely managing to pull Raquel into the kitchen before the roof sliced down past the edge of the floor like a guillotine, nearly cutting her in half. Turning back, she watched as the beams of the roof buckled and broke upon impact, the fallen half of the house finally collapsing in on itself in a plume of dust.

"Thanks," she managed to gasp, wide-eyed. She turned back to look at 49, who was staring into her eyes and even though he had just saved her, the expression on his face was unsettling. Holding both hope and shock, his golden eyes and silver face peered into hers like the face of some angel or devil. She didn't know it at the time, but she would soon find that she was right to be unsettled.

———

LESS THAN A MINUTE after the house had split in two, armed PUC soldiers had busted in the door and leveled their weapons at the scared and panting faces of Ritz, King, and all the rest. Ritz briefly considered going for his gun, but the chances of a stray round flying past him—or *through* him for that matter—were relatively high. This wouldn't have been a problem if everyone currently in his charge wasn't placed directly behind him, but as it stood he kept his gun holstered.

"On the ground," the lead soldier barked, jabbing his gun forward. Ritz and the others raised their hands and slowly spread out belly-down on the dusty kitchen floor.

"What the fuck is this thing?" one of the other soldiers said, walking up to 49, his gun raised.

"Not sure," the first one said, "maybe you should just kill it to be safe."

The second soldier appeared to be giving the idea genuine consideration, raising the barrel of his weapon up to 49's expressionless face. A beat of tension passed and then the barrel was lowered again.

"Kinsey. Barnes." The soldier shouted the two names and looked back toward the blasted doorframe. Two more soldiers hustled inside, weapons tilted downward. "Bring this synthetic to the prisoner processing station. Tell them I sent him to have his data downloaded."

Ritz let out a barely audible sigh, just loud enough for the soldier to hear and was rewarded with a tight little smile.

Good. He thought. *Let them think 49 is important.* The captain wasn't sure of 49's fighting capabilities in his current state, but he figured that the android would fare better facing two soldiers alone than he would facing ten while also surrounded by a group of children.

After securing a pair of metal manacles to the android's wrists and escorting him out, the other soldiers zip-tied Ritz's and the rest of the prisoners' hands together, right down to the youngest of the Jackson kids. They were then hauled down the street at gunpoint. All around them people were being marched along with guns at their backs, those who resisted being beaten and dragged.

"Where are they taking us?" asked one of the young Jackson boys; Ritz thought his name might have been Cory. The kid had a perpetually wide-eyed look about him that made him seem as if he were constantly discovering everything for the first time.

"We're just going to the center of town," Ritz said reassuringly. A few of the older Jackson kids shot him a distrusting stare but he ignored them. "They can't have anyone sneaking up on them in the middle of the night so they're just going to get us all in one place where they can keep an eye on us while they figure things out. Cool?"

The boy didn't look like he bought it exactly, but the interaction seemed to reassure him nonetheless.

Ritz breathed through his nostrils. Now if only he could reassure *himself*. In truth, he had no idea what was going to happen to them. He tried to adjust his arms behind his back, the hard plastic of the zip-ties biting into his skin. The guy who had pulled the tie had yanked on it as if he was trying to win a tug o' war contest, and if that was any indication of how lenient the PUC would be here then they were in for a rough ride.

Byzzie, who was a few feet up toward the front of the line overheard the exchange and dropped back. "And what if they execute us in the center of town?" she said out of the side of her mouth, just loud enough for Ritz to hear.

The captain shrugged. "Then we don't have to go be executed somewhere else," he said, just as quietly.

———

IF THE PUC had been planning any executions they had either changed their minds or were saving them for later. The Leopold and Jackson clan were marched into the center of town where they were huddled into hastily thrown-up cages. In the short amount of time it had taken them to seize control of Desia, the PUC had already constructed rows of electrified fencing up and down streets, sectioning them off into squares where prisoners could be densely packed inside.

Ritz watched as what looked like a large family of at least fifteen people struggled to press in on themselves to keep those on the outer edges from touching the wire. The young and the old seemed to make up those who existed in the center of the huddle while the healthier adults stood facing inward.

One woman—looking to be roughly 40 years of age—shifted just a hair-too-much and Ritz watched her yelp and jump as a crack of electricity sliced through the air. Hopping and trying to get away, the crowd jostled and churned and a few more cracks and cries of pain could be heard from the other side.

Ritz turned away.

Ritz's group was marched down to the last cage at the end of a row, and when they got there, the captain was dismayed to find five people already in the cage.

Should have given up sooner, he thought to himself. *At least then we could have gotten a more spacious holding cell.*

The two soldiers that had first knocked down the door of

the Jackson house were the ones leading this particular unwilling parade, and as they reached the doors, one of them—the one who had zip-tied Ritz's hands—reached up and keyed in a code. The lock on the door clacked upward and the other soldier stepped up to open it wide.

After filing into the tight little area, the door snapping shut behind them, Ritz followed the example of the family he had observed and urged his crew to take positions on the outer edges so that the younger of their group didn't have to stand next to the buzzing wires. The four others who had already been in the cage seemed somewhat reluctant to do the same, but after one of them—a large man with a salt and pepper beard—looked at the battle-hardened adults and teary-eyed children he quickly acquiesced, the others following suit.

Ritz himself was on the furthest edge of the cell and had to shrug his shoulders together and lean slightly inward to avoid the electric wires. The position he achieved was just manageable, but he wasn't sure he'd be able to hold it for long. He gently twisted his hands in back, feeling the hard plastic dig into his skin. His hands had begun to go numb, but he thought he might be able to figure out a way to shock some life into them, freeing himself in the process.

But the timing would need to be just right.

———

VANESSA JACKSON DID her best not to react when the Minister of Defense himself walked into her holding cell. The room was cramped and stuffy with a plain 3x5 foot aluminum table in the center. Unlike the polymer zip-ties she had seen on some of the other prisoners, Vanessa had had her hands secured in front of her by two large steel manacles, the cuffs of which were so big they dug into both the middle of her forearms up top and just below her thumbs on the bottom. The manacles were secured by two chains that met at the fork of a single chain and then wound through a giant steel loop bolted to the floor at Vanessa's feet. She didn't even try straining against it; she knew it was secure—she knew because she had built this room with her own two hands, yanking and testing the chains and bolts when it was all finished.

Despite being the Head of Desia's Defense Fleet, Vanessa never would have suspected she'd be getting interrogated by the infamous Seamus Clark himself, current Minister of Defense and heir to the PUC Surgical Equalizing Unit Program. Feeling a trickle of sweat roll down between her shoulder blades, she thought she had been able to maintain something resembling an air of composure, but she couldn't be sure.

Looking practically exuberant with energy, the compact military figure sat down in the chair across from her and motioned for the guard outside to close the door. When the door clanged shut, Clark leaned back and looked Vanessa in the eye, satisfaction plain on his weathered face.

"Your frigates didn't put up much of a fight," he said. "I half-expected to have a bloodbath on my hands, but except for a few stubborn ships and gun-operators, your people practically handed the Pillon System over." He shifted in his seat. "It's almost as if they *wanted* to be under PUC command."

Vanessa fixed his gaze, fighting to stay calm. She knew he was baiting her but it was hard not to take it all the same —to snap and reveal all of her insecurities in a single fatal second.

"Desia has a voluntary defense force," she said coolly.

"Most of the people employed come on to learn a skill and earn a paycheck, and some of them feel that that bounds them to a certain duty."

"But not all."

"Not even most," Vanessa said, stating the fact simply. "Most are just here to escape—to find some semblance of peace in a universe that has kicked them to the curb. People taking shelter in the Pillon System have come here because they've been ostracized by the PUC in some way. Sure, your laws and policies help some people. Hell, let's be overly generous and say that they help *most* people." She shook her head. "Still, a law will always put someone in the margin. There will always be the outlier that gets ground beneath the wheels of progress."

"I'm not following," Clark said, though his face told a different story. This was obviously an argument he had heard a hundred times before and he just wanted to hurry through the motions of letting Vanessa say her piece so they could move on.

"The Pillon System is a home for those outliers. A necessary neutral system that can house and support people pushed to the margins."

"And?"

"And," she said, failing to keep a bit of bite from her voice. "You might think you understand what you're doing—and maybe you even do on some sort of theoretical level—but you don't. Not wholly. Not bodily."

"Bodily?" Clark asked, raising an eyebrow. This time he actually did seem to be confused.

Vanessa leaned in. "What I'm saying is, maybe you can save 99 people by killing, shackling, and oppressing one. But until you've felt that oppression—that violence—then you'll never understand the full implications of what you're doing.

Not totally. Not *responsibly*. You may think you know what you're doing but that level of violence always rebounds."

"But that's my job now, isn't it?" Clark tilted his head to the side. "I have to enforce those rules or—if we're sticking to the analogy—the whole 100 die. The world is a violent place and if we don't impose some sort of order on it then the entire interplanetary system will devour itself in chaos."

Vanessa reached up to rub the back of her neck but was quickly reminded of her current position when the chain snapped tight, her hands only halfway raised to her face. She lowered them back down, breathing out a sigh of defeat.

"You can hold the entire world in your hands," she said softly. "But if you try and squeeze it too tight, I think you'll find it's a lot more dangerous and unyielding than even you."

Clark leaned in, dropping his voice for effect. "That's why I'm giving you a chance, Vanessa. You see, I don't want to—" he fluttered his hands lightly "—*squeeze the world* as you put it. In fact, if I had it my way, I wouldn't even have to raise a finger."

Vanessa remained silent. The man was clearly on a roll now and he'd get to the point with or without her interjection.

Clark leaned back again, reaching up to pull on the lapels of his uniform. "In about thirty minutes, I'm going to be walking through the doors of a secret facility just ten miles south of here and I'm going to flip a switch. And when I do, the Pillon System will be the last barbaric hold-out to be dragged into a more enlightened age—a more connected one."

Vanessa couldn't hold back her reaction this time and the look of alarm must have shown plainly on her face because she watched Clark practically laugh with satisfaction. "What are you saying?" She asked hesitantly, though she thought she had an idea.

No, she thought to herself. *Not already. They should have had more time.*

"The Light Wire is fully constructed," said the minister, confirming her fears. "It is fully constructed and operational and all it needs is an input code from yours truly and the Pillon System will finally be connected to the rest of the world."

"But we *are* connected to the rest of the world," Vanessa shouted, unable to contain herself any longer. "That's the whole *point*. We've always been connected. Our actions have always affected you and your actions have always affected us. That's how the world *works*. We *do* communicate with other systems. We speak and pass information just like anyone else. What you're talking about isn't connection, it's a monopoly on information. It's tyranny and control."

"And how else would you like me to stem the tide of vitriol and misinformation that is constantly *gushing* from this backwards little world you live on?" This time it was Clark who was unable to keep the scorn from his voice. "Do you know that one month ago four refinery workers on Onyx bludgeoned a woman to death thirty-five feet from her own home? When they were questioned after the incident, do you know what their excuse was?"

Vanessa felt her heart sink. Of course, she knew what the reason was. The story had played on every news network for a week straight at the time and she doubted there wasn't a single person in the entire planetary system that hadn't heard, but she let him tell it anyway.

"They killed her because of a recent unauthorized news bulletin written by a man named Dennis Plaine, living here in Glenhold. In *this very city*. It stated—and I quote: 'It is interesting to note that those who are in synthetic research and development are often of Asian descent.'" Clark slammed his hand down on the table, causing Vanessa to jump in her seat. "The woman they killed owned a fucking grocery store. Maybe it's not me who needs to watch how they're inflicting their will on the world, Vanessa. Maybe you need to take a little goddam responsibility for it yourself."

Vanessa didn't know what to say. While it was technically true that a lot of the leading scientists in the R & D sections of synthetics were of Korean descent, Plaine's statement had obviously been a thinly-veiled racial attack that had then lead to a racially-motivated crime on a planet destabilized by the friction between human and machine labor. The news article had been equal-parts hateful and irresponsible and when it had been traced back to a militant faction on Desia, Vanessa had felt a deep stab of shame.

The whole reason she had taken the job of Fleet Command on Desia had been to provide people with shelter and refuge, but what the man across from her was saying was true. The Pillon System was also a home for militants and insurgents. Some of them fought honorably to create a new world while others simply lashed out at people they despised. Some used this safe haven as a removed outpost from which they could spill hateful rhetoric.

"I am deeply sorry for some of the things our citizens do," Vanessa finally said. "But it's not for me or anyone to say what free people should do. That's the point." She tilted her head. "And I can guarantee you that you will not be hauling Mr. Plaine into custody."

"Oh? Are you going to defend his precious freedom

regardless of how much you disagree with him?" His voice was mocking.

"You will not be arresting him because he's already dead."

This caught Clark off guard but he recovered quickly. "So I see you take care of dissenting opinions the same way we do."

Vanessa shook her head. "We don't know who killed him. But one week ago, he and four other people who he had been living with turned up dead. Butchered. The place was so torn up that there could have been anywhere between four and forty people in there carving those men up. But the point is: that man knew what he was doing and the possible consequences. And he paid for them."

"And that makes it okay?"

"None of it's okay. What I'm saying is, he's an outlier. Most of us just want to be left alone. We want to work and come home to our families at night. That much should be obvious considering how many people fled the moment you showed up. They don't want to fight or *stick it to the man* or anything. They just want peace."

"Well," Clark said, lifting his wrist to look at his watch. He dropped his arm back down again. "I'm going to give you a chance to let them have that peace."

"Mmmmhmmm."

Clark laughed. "I'm serious Vanessa, this is your one shot."

"And what do I have to do? Sacrifice my firstborn on live television or something?"

"Quite the opposite," Clark said. "In fact, if you do what I say, Byzantine's record will be wiped clean."

Vanessa felt her heart clench.

"Oh yes, of course we know of your connection to Byzantine Jackson, infamous crewmate of known thieves and murderers. Do you know they stole a *Light Core* from that base they wrecked? A Light Core. Those aren't cheap and neither were the lives of the men and women they killed—men and women who will never get to go home to *their* families."

A heavy silence permeated the room as Vanessa looked on. The ideological debate was clearly over. Now it was time for dealing. Leveraging. She just wished she knew how much she was willing to give up, because when it came right down to it, her heart would have her set Desia on fire if it meant saving one of her children. If she let it, that was.

"All you need to do is say that you agreed to set up the Light Wire on Desia," Clark said, as if it were nothing more than picking up a gallon of milk at the grocery store.

"Why me?" she asked. "Surely there are more influential people in the Pillon System."

"Not here," he said. "You have an image with these people. Nothing in this city escapes your notice. I know I could ask you for every name associated with the murder of Dennis Plaine and, while you might not *want* to give them to me, you'd at least know them. Desia has no President—no Prime Minister. All they have is a volunteer defense force and you are at the head of it. You're the closest thing these people have to a leader Ms. Jackson."

"It's Mrs. Jackson, thank you. And I'm not these people's leader. They lead themselves."

"Regardless," Clark held up a hand. "Your word goes a long way."

"So what? I'd just get up and endorse you? Is that it? Say —yeah a massive military naval fleet just knocked down the fucking door and killed a bunch of people in the streets, but it was all in the plan. They're good guys. No need to worry. Something like that?"

"Desia is home to Kingsbane," the minister explained, as if she were hearing this for the first time. "Kingsbane is one of the largest militant insurgent groups in all of interplanetary space. I'll give a short speech and then flip the switch. Then all you have to do is say that they took control and pulled Desian forces into a battle that they weren't prepared for and a lot of innocent people died in the process. It's sad. It's unfortunate. But it's taken care of. Then we move on with the endorsement."

"And if I do this, you'll wipe my daughter's record?" Vanessa asked.

Clark nodded.

Good, she thought. If he knew she was here on this planet they'd be negotiating for Byzzie's life, not her record. So at least there was that.

"Can I have some time to think on-"

"No," he cut her off. His face was suddenly stone. "You cannot. I'm leaving *now*." And to drive this fact home, he stood up.

Vanessa tried to stand up too but she hit the end of her chain and snapped back into the chair. Shit, she had to *think*. She needed more time.

"I'll do it," she blurted. "Clear Byzzie's name and I'll do it."

Clark's face was stone, betraying nothing.

"If you go back on this," he said, his voice made of solid ice. "I will kill you and every single person with the last name 'Jackson' living inside or outside PUC space. You understand?"

Vanessa nodded. She hadn't agreed in her heart yet. Not totally. She needed time and this was the best way to buy it.

There was nothing she could do sitting here in a cell. This way, at least she could keep her eyes open for any opportunities to turn the tables on Clark.

And she would. One way or another. Even if she got up on live TV and lied her heart out to all of her most-trusted allies, she had already decided that Seamus Clark was going to die. She didn't know how yet, but it was inevitable. He had stepped too far and if the death of Dennis Plaine had taught Vanessa anything it was that there was a price to pay for such things.

Seamus Clark had incurred a debt the moment he passed through that Void Gate with a whole fleet at his back. Now it was just a matter of time.

7

PRISONERS

When presented with his first chance to escape —a call over the comms that distracted not one but *both* of the men escorting him—49 did not take it. He could have gotten away, sure, but the location was all wrong. Standing smack-dab in the center of the city, soldiers and civilians hustling by in groups of no less than ten at a time, the chances of collateral damage were simply too high. And if the soldiers were that inattentive, they'd slip up again, and hopefully they'd be in a better spot at that point.

They did and they were.

"Where am I going?" 49 asked once the three of them were on the edge of town. His voice was calm. Non-threatening.

"There's a prisoner processing station just through the woods here," one of the soldiers said. He was young and walked with the sort of confidence an unconfident person got when they held a gun. From what he could tell from the two men's conversation, this one's name was Kinsey and the other, Barnes.

"A processing station?" he asked. "In the woods? That doesn't sound like an ideal location."

"We didn't have time to-" Kinsey began, but Barnes shot him a glance, immediately silencing him.

49 didn't need any more information. He understood. The blitz invasion of Desia had had a fair deal of planning put into it—where they would put the prisons, the interrogation rooms, and other things like that—but as with every operation, there were things they couldn't plan for. If 49 were to guess, he would bet that any number of outliers were being kept in this hastily established processing station. These soldiers and generals were used to dealing with two groups of people: enemies and allies.

But what happened when you found a diplomat or senator that wasn't supposed to be here? Or an activist group pushing for Desia to join the Light Wire Network and PUC controlled space? What happened when you found a glowing metallic android?

The processing station was likely just a holding cell for people that they didn't know what to do with. Those who couldn't be readily called enemies or allies. Chances were good it was also where they were downloading information from other non-combat synthetics in their never-ending war for information.

"What will happen to me?" 49 asked. He felt the metal manacles that secured his wrists behind him, testing their strength. The two men had to be in the exact right position for his plan to work.

At first, no one said anything. It was clear that neither of them was sure how to address this shiny *being* they had unexpectedly come across. If they treated him as an enemy soldier then they wouldn't talk to him due to protocol. And if they treated him like a docile synthetic, then they wouldn't talk to him because they'd see him as nothing more than a simple object—they'd treat him the way one might treat a fancy toaster.

But if he could let on that he had something they might want, they might be willing to break protocol. After all, if there was one thing that 49 had learned in his time dealing with humans, it was that the strictness of any rule could always be softened by a little selfish ambition...

"Is this where you brought the other Silver Assets?" 49 asked. He delivered the question nonchalantly, dangling the bait just within reach.

Barnes glanced back at him, his pace slowing. Kinsey slowed down to match his partner. 49 wanted to push further but he let the silence hang, staring straight ahead.

Barnes finally broke. "The Silver Assets," he said carefully. "What is their purpose?" The question was simple and direct, stated the same way someone might type a command into an AI terminal.

"The purpose of all Silver Assets is to safeguard sensitive militia intelligence. If one is captured, protocol is to wipe all memory."

The two soldiers abruptly came to a halt. Kinsey looked over at Barnes, the two of them visibly excited. 49 could almost see the reel of promotions and commendations playing through the two soldiers' heads.

"Did you wipe your memory when you were captured?" Kinsey asked. The crucial question.

"Negative," 49 replied. The two men were close to him, but not close enough. Not yet. "Captain Tariq was in the process of inputting rendezvous coordinates. Any input process overrides the memory wipe command."

The look on Barnes' face immediately became that of someone who had just struck gold. His neck was flushed, his posture wobbly. A sheen of sweat had broken out on his face. He stepped forward.

"Where are the rest of-" he began to ask, but just as he got within range, 49 snapped the steel manacles behind him and brought his hands around in a lightning-fast blur of silver. He leaned in just a bit, and was able to grab each of the men's rifles. Before they could react, the powerful android had crushed both of the weapon's receivers and tossed them aside.

Kinsey tried to run first and 49 brought him down with a quick backhand. The strike hit him just upside the head and as the man crumpled, Barnes lunged backward, cleared his holster, and tried to bring his sidearm up. He wasn't fast enough.

In a split-second, 49 rushed forward and grabbed the pistol from the man's hand. He squeezed again, crushing the weapon. This time however, the sound of snapping bones pierced the air as the man's fingers broke and came apart in the android's grip. The soldier opened his mouth to scream, but before he could, 49 landed a blow on the right side of his head. He dropped unconscious to the ground beside his friend.

49 looked around. The tight forest trail stood still and empty around him, the hidden jungle creatures holding their breath in silence. There was no one else in the area.

After dragging the two unconscious bodies out of sight, 49 began to run toward the prisoner processing facility.

———

WHILE 49 TOOK down his two captors, Ritz was planning his own escape. There wasn't much he could do from inside the cage, even if he managed to free his hands out from behind him. The crucial point would occur the next time the soldiers opened the gate. He was fairly certain he could melt the plastic zip-tie by pressing it against the fence behind him. It would hurt like hell and he'd probably fry all of the nerves in his hand, but if the small shocks the other prisoners were getting were any indication, the voltage wouldn't be enough to knock him down.

From there, he'd rush the guard, grab him, and use him as a human shield while he pulled the man's sidearm from his holster. The guard would probably have his rifle shouldered over his back, and he'd be able to hand that off to King while the rest of the prisoners filtered out behind him.

King would be the problem here. Byzzie and Raquel would hesitate but they'd do the right thing in the end. They'd run into the woods and escape while Ritz stayed behind. It'd be a tough decision but there could be no second-guessing with Byzzie's family on the line. They'd get one shot at this.

However, with how hard King had taken Hector's death, there was no telling how he would react. Hector, Ritz, and King had been the core members of the Leopold. Before Byzzie or the Marauders or anyone else, there had been the three of them. Now with Hector gone, King would be loath to abandon his last real friend in the world.

He would have to deal with it though. This was the situation and there was nothing they could do to change it. The group that would be escaping stood the best chance with King alongside them. He was the most seasoned of the crew, even more than Ritz, and his knowledge and experience would be invaluable.

Ritz had just begun to consider what it would mean for King to stay with him—to die with him, most likely—when a trio of soldiers rounded the corner, dragging a young man by the hair.

The prisoner was more of a boy than a man, and judging by the expression on the soldiers' faces, it was obvious that he had already been a handful. The boy screamed and kicked his legs as he was dragged, his hands clamped tightly around the soldier's grip on his hair. He was bleeding from his forehead, and it was hard to tell if it was because of how he was being dragged or if he had already been cracked by the butt of a rifle.

There were three soldiers in all: the one dragging him and two others walking behind with their guns trained on the prisoner.

"Marcel!" shouted a woman behind Ritz. The noise was startling and Ritz turned to see the look of anguish on the woman's face. She tried to dart forward, but only ended up sending a number of other prisoners—including Ritz—bouncing and sparking off of the fences.

As he recovered, the back of his arms tingling where they had been fried, Ritz saw the grizzled grey-haired man wrap his arms around the woman. At first, he thought it might be to keep her from repeating her actions, but then Ritz saw the look of pain on her face mirrored on his, and it became obvious that the young man was their son.

When the trio of soldiers made it to the gate where Ritz and the others were being held, the woman's son was hurled into the dirt by the man dragging him. He then immediately sprung up and charged the three men, only to be clobbered across the face by the leading man's rifle. The woman behind Ritz sobbed, but remained still.

"Don't hurt him," the grey-haired man begged. "Just throw him in here and he won't bother you anymore."

"I'm not going in a fucking cage," the kid spat through his bleeding mouth. "I said 'never' and I mean it."

"Stop it, Marcel," the grey-haired man snarled. "Grow up. I don't care what those-" The man stopped himself and changed tactics. "Just please, join your mother and me. This will all be sorted out."

Never accept a cage, Ritz thought to himself. That was what the boy had been referring to. It was the motto of the militant separatist group named Kingsbane, and he prayed that the other soldiers hadn't caught the reference, because if they had, then Marcel would be executed right here.

"There is no greater prison than your own mind," Ritz cut in and saw the kid stop. He turned and looked at him, assessing.

Ritz tried to project his greatest air of authority. It was clear that Marcel had recognized the quote. It was one commonly said by members of Kingsbane, but far lesser known to the public. He had taken a chance by using it, but judging by the looks on the soldiers' faces they didn't recognize it for what it was. Marcel, on the other hand, did, and that was what was important.

If Ritz could somehow convince the young man that he was a part of Kingsbane—he actually had been at one time, before he could no longer stomach their methods—then he might just be able to show the kid that there was no shame in refusing to die a pointless death.

The look on the young man's face began to soften, and Ritz almost felt the woman at his back tense with hope— hope that her son might actually listen to reason. Hope that she wouldn't have to see him die today.

"Get the fuck in there," yelled the man who had been dragging him, drawing a black automatic pistol from his holster. The soldier used it to backhand Marcel across the face. Blood sprayed as the front sight carved a deep groove in his cheek. The kid staggered and then bounced off of the fence with a loud crack of electricity.

A scream of sheer guttural rage ripped out of Marcel's throat, and then he threw himself at the soldier who had struck him. The soldier tried to strike him again, but this time Marcel caught the gun in his hands and tried wrenching it out.

"Drop it!" One of the other soldiers yelled as he raised his rifle. The two struggling men fought lurching from side to side, each of them fighting for control of the gun. Marcel leaned back on his right leg and tried to throw his attacker into the electric fence but the man was too big. Instead, the soldier reversed the maneuver and threw Marcel. Marcel, for his part, managed to maintain his grip on the soldier's hand and dragged him back with him. Electricity crackled and spat as the two men fried on the fence, the gun falling to the ground.

Marcel was the first one back up, but before he could do anything else, one of the soldiers behind him fired a single shot through his right thigh.

A cry of pain pierced the air, combined with twin cries of anguish from his parents. Ritz felt his stomach drop as he looked on helplessly.

The kid had fallen to his knees and remained there as the soldier who had fired the shot came up behind him and grabbed him by the hair again.

"No," said the leader, wiping his mouth. Anger blazed in his eyes. "Step back."

The other soldier hesitated for only a second and then did as he was told. Ritz saw what was coming and immediately began trying to find a way to stop it.

"What was that about cages you said earlier?" the soldier

said. "You know, we have a 'shoot on-site' order for any self-proclaimed members of known terrorist organizations." He bent down and picked up his fallen sidearm, shaking the dust off of it.

He was close, Ritz thought to himself, but was he close enough? There was an electrified post on the left side of the gate door and that would be the key. The holes in the fence itself were too small, but the supporting beams that stood at each corner and on either side of the gate had just enough room between them and the wire to fit his hands. He wasn't sure if he'd be able to take the shock for that long though. Only one way to find out.

He just hoped he was doing the right thing.

The soldier raised the barrel of his weapon to the kid's face, and Ritz heard the woman behind him wail. Before he could pull the trigger however, Ritz deftly hopped into the air, swinging his bound wrists underneath him and bringing them out in front. It was a maneuver he had had to practice in his short time in Kingsbane, but he had never forgotten it. He was even lucky enough to avoid touching the fence itself, though he did knock into some people behind him and heard a few cries from the back as the motion rippled through the crowd and some of the prisoners were forced into the fence.

By that time however, Ritz had already thrust his hands against the electrified post, melting the zip-ties and immediately thrusting his hands through. The electricity burned his skin and coursed through him. He could already feel the dexterity leaving his fingers, but all he needed to do was clamp down.

His sudden movement had been enough to faze the soldiers and they had already begun to turn their heads toward him by the time he was pressing his wrists against the post. This delay gave the boy just enough time to fall sideways to the ground, effectively saving his life.

With a herculean effort, Ritz clamped his hands down on the soldier's forearm, sending at least 1,000 volts of electricity into his body. The gun cracked in his hand as he involuntarily fired and, with a final burst of strength, Ritz pulled the man into the electric fence, both of their faces mashing against the wire.

It felt like he was being simultaneously frozen and lit on fire. Electricity surged through him, smoke filling the air along with a number of screams. It wasn't exactly how Ritz had intended on going out and this definitely didn't help the Jackson family or his crew. But he couldn't take it—couldn't stand watching that boy be executed right here in front of his family.

When Ritz had been a child he had experienced something similar, and it had warped him for the rest of his life. Shaped him and spurred him with anger. In a single act, he had lost his home and his family and his faith. The boy he had been was effectively destroyed. So however calculated his original plans of escape had been, as soon as the man had raised the gun to that boy's head, Ritz had been damned to this path of action.

The Jackson family was doomed. The Leopold was doomed. Their entire mission was doomed, but at least he could wrap this man in an embrace and use his hatred to literally burn the life from his body. Stars and darkness began to climb up into his vision and, in those fleeting seconds, he just hoped that the boy would be able to escape in the confusion. He hoped that somehow, he would buy him just enough time to escape into the woods.

He didn't. Of course, he didn't.

———

RAQUEL WATCHED in horror as the entire sequence of events took place. The boy being dragged into view by his hair. The captain electrocuting the man on the fence along with himself. All of it. She wanted to grab Ritz herself and yank him away. Almost did, actually, but something stopped her. This was his decision, and what would happen if she intervened?

Most likely: the soldier would live and Ritz would be shot on the spot. It would be worthless. The entire thing—the crew, the invasion, her *life*—it would all be worthless. The crushing feeling of helplessness overwhelmed her, and then it doubled when she watched the boy die.

In the confusion, he had tried scrabbling away on his hands and knees. It may have even worked if the soldiers had been different people—if they had focused more on freeing their leader than taking care of the boy. But they weren't.

The one who had shot the boy in the leg quickly stepped forward as he was crawling away, booted him in the side, and then fired a quick burst from his energy rifle into his back. The boy's mother was just to Raquel's left, and she let out a heart-wrenching scream. She flew into motion, trying to push her way forward. Frightened people around her hopped and jostled, trying to stay still but it was in vain. Soon enough, the entire cell of prisoners was rocking back and forth to the sound of people sparking off of the fences.

As this was happening, the other soldier carefully kicked his leader away from the fence and once he was clear, the man raised his rifle and fired.

At first, Raquel wasn't sure what had happened.

The first thing she saw was the flash of gunfire, followed

by Ritz collapsing sideways onto the ground. Raquel's heart froze in her chest, and that was when she noticed two other things. It had become quiet and there was something wet and warm running down her face.

Slowly, almost as if in a trance, Raquel reached up to touch the left side of her cheek.

Somewhere in the back of her mind, she acknowledged King and Byzzie pushing their way through the crowd to get to their captain. She acknowledged them rolling him over and the look on Byzzie's face as she searched for a pulse, King already stripping off his shirt to use as a bandage to staunch the bleeding. She saw all of this, and somewhere deep inside of her, she felt a small spark of hope.

All of that was pushed to the background however. All Raquel could focus on at the moment were the bits of blood and bone and brain matter on the side of her face. And the fact that the screaming beside her had abruptly ceased.

8

COUNTING DOWN

The building where they were processing prisoners was little more than a small three-room outbuilding used to house workers for a nearby power plant. There were two guards posted out front and it was obvious from the noise coming from within that there were far more people inside than the building was designed to hold.

49 watched from behind a tree for a few minutes, hoping that the black robe he was wearing was doing enough to obscure whatever glow the transformed Light Core inside of him might be giving off. It was still broad daylight, so he certainly fared better than if he had tried walking around in the pitch black, but he didn't want to take too many chances. What he needed right now was information and the sooner he could get it, the better.

His chance came relatively soon when the front door swung open to reveal what looked to be a rear admiral, judging by her uniform. The woman was tall with a large frame and a rigid face that looked as if it could have been carved from stone. What was most concerning, however, was how she flexed her right hand and removed a pair of brass knuckles to wipe away a small spatter of blood from her bruised hand.

In a single moment, 49 reassessed the information he had. This prisoner processing center wasn't a center to sort out anomalies and diplomats. This was an interrogation room and the kind of "processing" they were doing probably involved a lot fewer questions and a lot more broken bones.

The PUC had come into power long after 49 had disappeared into the Void onboard the Mary, but from what he had gathered from Ritz and the others, places like this existed everywhere in PUC controlled space. And while they may not have been a secret, they also weren't exactly brought up in campaign speeches either. This was just one more thing to add into 49's assessment of the PUC's attack on Desia and the conclusion he came to wasn't a pretty one.

They were obviously here for a singular purpose and whatever it was, they weren't planning on leaving any time soon. This was no scouting mission on the Desian capital or slash and burn hunt for militia groups. This was an invasion and unless they were thrown out, the PUC would own this entire planet.

The admiral chatted with the guards for a few seconds, lighting a cigarette as she spoke. The two men next to her looked stiff, as if they were engaging with her as minimally as possible. She was either used to it or didn't care, however, because she continued on as if they weren't terrified to misstep and she eventually finished her cigarette, ground it out in the dirt beneath her heel, and then turned to walk back inside.

49 sprang into motion and didn't slow down until three people were unconscious and he was a mile away.

———

Vanessa rode to the Light Wire between two heavily armed soldiers in the back seat of a large all-terrain vehicle. She couldn't tell how long the convoy was, but it looked like there was a CSDV, or Combat Synthetic Deployment Vehicle, traveling down the thin paved road directly in front of them.

She was outnumbered and outgunned to the point where something like escape was about as likely as a giant ice cream cone falling out of the sky to crush whatever vehicle Minister Clark was traveling in. She worked through it in her head and then worked through it again. She was traveling to the Light Wire where they'd probably be setting up television crews at that very moment. They'd either make her watch and smile while Clark threw the switch or make her do it herself. Then she'd have to look into the cameras and compromise every value she'd ever held.

Was it worth it? She would be saving her daughter's future, but the question wasn't simple for her. She'd lived and breathed Desia her entire life—the air, the mishmash of cultures, the people, all of it—and while her gut reaction was to save her daughter at all costs, some part of her resisted it. She couldn't just betray all of these people— couldn't get up there and effectively obliterate their faith in her and everything she stood for in a single broadcast.

Time was running out, however, and after the convoy had stopped and she found herself walking into the Light Wire facility that had been secretly constructed in her back- yard, she was no closer to landing on an answer. So instead of dwelling on it, she put it out of her mind. She closed her eyes briefly and let the spirits of Desia and her ancestors guide her.

When the time came she would make a decision.

———

"WHAT DO YOU NEED?" Raquel asked in a panic. It had taken her a few precious moments to get over the shock of having someone's head explode against the side of her face, but as soon as King started bellowing orders, she quickly dropped into emergency mode.

"Raquel, I need your fingers. Byzzie, see if you can make some space." King had climbed one-leg-after-the-other through his bound arms so he could hold his hands out in front and then immediately pressed his wrist against the fence post the same way Ritz had to melt the zip-ties. Everyone in the pen looked either shocked or scared, especially the man who had just witnessed both his wife and son get murdered in the last thirty seconds and was now kneeling on the ground, the expression on his face rapidly fluctuating between bewilderment and sheer devastation.

At the sound of the gunfire, four more soldiers had come dashing down the line of electrified cells, rifles at the ready. After quickly taking in the situation, two of them had hoisted up the unconscious captain that Ritz had tried immolating with the fence. The other soldiers looked wearily around and began to follow the others. The one who had shot Ritz saw that King had freed himself, but didn't seem to be too worried about it seeing as he was still locked up. Still, it was clear that he was making a mental note that there was a prisoner inside that was no longer secured and could possibly try fighting his way out when they finally decided to move them.

"He's in bad shape," King said. "One of the rounds grazed his shoulder and another went wide, but he took one shot right in the chest." King rolled Ritz onto his side and Raquel saw what he meant. On the right side of the captain's chest was a puckered blood-soaked hole.

While King worked on Ritz, Byzzie tried to clear some room. Some of the prisoners were able to back up a bit, but now that there were two whole bodies laying on the ground plus the man sobbing over his dead wife, there wasn't a whole lot of space in what had already been pretty tight quarters. Then Cory, one of Byzzie's brothers, had an idea.

"Get on each other's shoulders," he said. He spoke directly to his siblings, and at first they were hesitant. Then, his hands still bound, he nodded at one of his little sisters and then nodded at an older brother that looked as if they could bear the weight of the child on their shoulders. It was touch and go for a few seconds as the two wobbled around trying to position themselves just right, but eventually, with the help of the others, the young girl Cory had pointed at had her tiny legs wrapped around her older brother's neck.

"Does anyone have a plastic bag or tape?" King yelled as the rest of the Jackson family tried the same maneuver.

"I've always got tape," said Byzzie. At first, she tried to reach down into the side pocket of her cargo pants but couldn't quite reach with the zip-ties, so she eventually walked over to where King was kneeling and thrust her leg out at him. He quickly flipped up the velcro flap, reached inside, and pulled out a small roll of electrical tape.

"This'll work," he said. "Raquel, I need you. Free your hands."

Raquel hesitated. She had seen what the fence could do to someone and it didn't exactly look like something she wanted to experience.

"Now," King shouted, and before she could spend any

more time thinking about it, she backed up to the fence and thrust the plastic ties against the electrified wire.

The pain was nothing she could have prepared for. It felt like stinging hornets were racing through her entire body, paralyzing her muscles in the process. At first, the pain was so intense that she didn't even succeed at melting the ties all the way and she had to try a second time. She got it on the next try though and then hustled over to King.

"Hold this tight while I tape the ends," King said. He had pulled a piece of waxy paper out of his pocket and was smoothing it over on Ritz's wound.

"Is that from your cheeseburger last night?"

"It's what I got, okay?" he said defensively. "Now hold it down."

Raquel did as she was asked and held the piece of paper over the wound. There was a lot of blood but she had seen worse, which she figured was a good sign. Ritz, however, looked far from good. Eyes closed and chest heaving, he kept taking spasmodic breaths and twisting his body, making it hard to keep the wax paper on.

"His lung is collapsing," King said. "Make sure that he stays on his side so the wound stays open."

While Raquel pressed the makeshift bandage to Ritz's chest, King quickly wiped away the blood from the wound with a piece of his shirt and then began taping the sides of the paper until they were secure on all edges except for the upper left-hand corner.

"Keep your hand there," he instructed. "Don't press too hard or the air stuck inside of his chest won't get out, but make sure to press hard enough to where there isn't any getting in either."

Raquel nodded as she switched hands, making sure she

kept a firm amount of pressure on the wound. Ritz's breathing slowly began to even out.

He looked bad though. His face was pale and his skin was clammy. Despite the makeshift bandage King had made for him, it was clear that if he didn't get a doctor soon, he would die. Raquel looked around from the inside of the cage but there was no one. Except for the other prisoners, they were on their own.

———

VANESSA STOOD ON THE PLATFORM, unable to keep her jaw from dropping at the sight of the massive internal structure of the Light Wire. The procession of soldiers had first made their way through a tight hallway lined with tiny offices, but soon they had come to the interior of the facility, which was a wide-open room with a giant dome overhead made out of thick diamond-reinforced glass. In the center of the room was a thick silver spire roped with thick glowing cords of golden light. At the base of the spire was a giant computer panel with a huge manual throw switch bolted on.

"Does that switch actually work?" Vanessa asked hesitantly as she walked down a small flight of steps to the base of the spire. There were two armed soldiers at her back, plus another ten or so spaced throughout the room. A camera crew was setting up on a small platform adjacent to the base, and Minster Clark was standing a foot away from the throw switch, looking the mechanism over.

"Of course it doesn't," he answered. "No one has ever made history by punching in a short string of code on a computer screen though."

Vanessa thought that there probably *had* been some people who had gone down in history that way, but she couldn't think of any off the top of her head and chose to remain silent. Instead, she looked around the room, trying to find a way out. She noticed a small exit near the south corner, but it was at best 50 feet away. And even if she made it, there was no telling how many people there were outside combing the streets and jungle.

It all seemed so hopeless.

"So how does this work?" she asked.

"You're going to come up here," Clark said, stepping aside, "And be in-frame as I throw the switch. Meanwhile, Nathan over there-" he pointed at a slightly balding man who was sitting behind a computer console, a camera crew, and what looked like an inch of bulletproof glass, "-is going to type in the initiation code at the same time and actually get the thing going. There's going to be a big whir of machinery. A lot of *oooohs* and *aaaaaaahs*. And then you're going to give a speech on unity and cooperation. You're going to endorse the PUC presence on Desia and denounce the violence caused by Kingsbane."

Vanessa nodded as she stepped up onto the platform where Clark was standing. Once she was next to him, he motioned her to spin around, and once she did, one of the soldiers who had been escorting her took an ancient-looking key from his pocket and unlocked her manacles. He then stepped back out of the shot.

"Almost forgot about those," she said morosely. "I guess that woulda ruined the take, huh?"

"Listen to me," Clark said. His voice was gentle but his hand drifted down to the holster on the right side of his hip. "There is no 'second take.' You have one shot at this. One shot for you, your daughter, and all of Desia. Do you understand?"

Vanessa gave the smallest of nods.

The whole thing was a gross violation of everything she believed in while also managing to be almost laughably theatrical. *Then again*, she thought as she looked around at the camera crew that was almost set up, *it does make for good TV.*

"We're ready when you are minister," called a well-groomed anchorwoman in a red blazer. She was standing with a microphone in her hand and Vanessa absentmindedly wondered if she had come here aboard the PUC vessels or if she had been here the whole time, a hungry predator waiting to pounce on a juicy story.

"Ok," Clark said, giving a thumbs up. Then he turned to Vanessa and raised his eyebrows. "*One shot*," he mouthed. Then he turned back around to face the cameras just as the cameraman counted down to one.

The cameras began to roll. And by the time they had stopped, Vanessa was pinned to the ground with five rifle barrels shoved in her face.

9

A SONG OVER THE RADIO

Lucas Clark tried to imagine the Light Wire facility on Desia. The sharp scent of fresh construction. Sterile and shining. Ready to be used. Silver hardware eager for light.

He probably figured it looked similar to the one he was in now. The cramped, utilitarian offices and hallways. The wide open room in the center. The massive spire looking like some great surgical needle ready to operate on the most vulnerable parts of the universe. Which was appropriate, Lucas thought to himself as he walked down the narrow hallway, because it was going to be used to excise the cancer of humanity from the face of existence.

After watching his father fight for years to make some sort of progress within the bureaucracy of the PUC, Lucas had had every ounce of faith in humanity's inherent goodness wiped away. His father had fought tooth and claw for a lasting peace in the galaxy and done so from one of the most powerful positions available. And what had that achieved? There were hate crimes in the Onyx System. There was hate speech coming from the Pillon System. And most of all, there was a bitter seed of hatred deep inside of his own heart. Lucas Clark lived in a state of privilege that afforded him a wide view of the universe, and all he could see was hatred permeating every inch of soil that mankind came in contact with.

His father thought that he could resist it—thought he could overcome it by simply doing good and fighting the noble fight. But in doing so he had become a jaded and embittered old man. Hate was a symptom of society, not something else. In no living species inhabiting the countless number of known planets of the universe could you find something approximating hate. Therefore, it stood to reason that hate was artificial. It was societal. It was unnatural. And most of all, it was human.

Everything Lucas had experienced and read about nature was serene and nurturing. It was about balance. It was the rightful order of being and mankind was nothing but a taint on its perfection. It was a disease in an otherwise healthy body.

And today would mark the first step of that disease being removed.

"Hey Lucas," someone called out from one of the rooms he was passing by.

Lucas stopped and stepped backward, poking his head around the corner and into the room. He was suddenly very conscious of the massive backpack hanging on his shoulders. Still though, he didn't want to seem suspicious. He was blending in. Acting natural. After all, he worked here. Today was just another day on the job.

He had made it through the metal detectors up front by sabotaging their sending and receiving software. He had talked his way past the guard, Trevor, by chatting with him about an upcoming dinner at the man's dreaded in-laws. No pat-down. No bag check.

And no dinner if all went accordingly.

The bag check was the main thing. Not only was his jerry-rigged transponder in there, but there was the other thing. The final thing. His final hope and salvation.

It should be any moment now. His father had left yesterday, and without saying as much, had in all likelihood been leaving for the invasion of Desia. That had to be it. No other way of explaining the man's serious yet exuberant attitude.

And if Lucas was wrong? Well then, no harm would be done. He still had his own plan. Was still operating on his own schedule. In reality, he could hijack the signal whenever he wanted.

But he wanted to do it now. Just like his father, he was watching all of his plans come together, and while he could wait another day or two, it was physically painful to do so.

"What's up?" Lucas asked, trying to mask his impatience. The man who had spoken to him was named Dmitri, a rail-thin 20-something with dark curly hair and a pale complexion. He was eating out of a bowl of popcorn while the small television jabbered in the corner.

"You see the news?" Dmitri asked. He gestured at the screen with a hand slick with salt and melted butter. "Someone tried to shoot your dad."

"What?" Lucas said, suddenly forgetting everything. "Who? When?"

"Just now on TV. I'm surprised you didn't see it."

Lucas was surprised that Dmitri *had* seen it. The invasion of Desia must have gone exceedingly well if they were already broadcasting. Even if the footage aired live, it would have only aired live across the Pillon System. The very nature of the Light Wire meant that truly live television couldn't be broadcast from system-to-system until the wire was operating.

With the exception of direct contact with his father, a news report on the situation was Lucas's queue to put the final step of his plan in motion. Sweat broke out on his forehead at the finality of it all. The speed at which it was happening. The backpack slung over his shoulder suddenly felt ten times heavier.

"Yeah, it was pretty incredible," Dmitri said. The break room was tight and grease-stained. The excited energy coming from the man almost seemed as if it was bouncing off of the cramped walls and out into the hallway. "They established a Light Wire on Desia. Your dad gave a short speech, then when he went to turn it on, some woman stopped him. She tried to grab his gun—almost had it too—but well, you know your dad. He certainly hasn't lost a step over the years."

"Wait," Lucas said, his head spinning. "Is he okay?" Then. "And the Light Wire is up? It's running?"

"Yup," Dmitri nodded vigorously. "The cameras cut out pretty quickly, but it looked like he was fine. The reporters say there's still a lot of fighting going on with the militia forces but with the facility already set up, the whole operation seemed to be pretty quick and successful."

Without saying another word, Lucas turned and began walking down the hall toward the spire. The last one was up. The time was now. He'd broadcast directly over the wire to his dad, and then he'd end this nightmare.

He'd end it all.

———

"You're dead, you bitch," Seamus Clark spat as he wound up and booted Vanessa Jackson in the ribs. The other soldiers who had initially brought her to the ground had stepped away but they still had their rifles up. "You're dead. And your daughter's dead. And everyone you've ever fucking met is dead."

He was furious. There was always the possibility that she would do something like this, but he thought he had had her figured out. She had been surrounded by armed soldiers. The Light Wire was being initiated whether she liked it or not. And he was holding her daughter's future ransom. She should have listened—should have obeyed. After all, what had she gained?

She had humiliated him on live TV and that was it. Granted, he was pissed, but at the end of the day he had still succeeded. Desia was his. The wire was up. Vanessa on the other hand? She'd be begging for death before the sun set.

"What did you think you were going to do, huh?" He leaned down as she rolled over on the floor. She was holding her ribs and gasping for breath. "Were you going to shoot me on live TV? Is that it? Start a civil war where billions of people die? What? Tell me."

The woman on the ground tried to suck in a lungful of air. She was bleeding from multiple scrapes on her face and forehead and Clark gave her another one with the toe of his boot. Her head snapped back and he watched her eyes roll into the back of her head as her eyelids fluttered closed.

He didn't know if she was dead or dying or just unconscious. No matter. It was all the same to him.

"It was rhetorical," he said to himself, trying to vent his anger. He should have been happy—should have been ecstatic actually—but the damn woman had stolen the moment from him. He had succeeded, true, but he was too busy wrestling her to the ground to enjoy it. One of the few great moments in his life had passed by before he could acknowledge it.

He turned around and began walking to the camera crew. He had to make sure they had no footage of the meltdown he had just had. If they had been broadcasting then they would continue broadcasting as he personally executed the entire crew on live television for all of Desia to see.

"Hey," he hollered at a stocky man who looked to be operating a large camera. "That thing on?"

The man looked suddenly nervous and Clark began to pick up his pace. Before he could get there, however, one of the soldiers called to him.

"Sir, we have an incoming transmission."

"What?" Clark stopped walking. "A transmission? From where?"

"From Lydia." The man tilted his head down, obviously listening to someone talking in his earpiece, "It's your son."

"What?" Clark said again, louder this time. He had removed his own earpiece before the broadcast and now dug frantically in his pocket trying to find it. Finally getting ahold of the small tan device, he pushed it into his ear and reached up to turn the small microphone attached to his lapel back on.

"Hello?" he said. "Who is this?"

At first, there was nothing and Clark began to wonder if he was dreaming. The whole day had been crazy. No less crazy than any other invasion he had conducted, but between the Jackson woman's attempt on his life on television and now one of his soldiers trying to convince him that his son had somehow keyed into the comms system, everything that was happening could just as easily have been a dream.

Then he spoke.

"Dad?" His voice was weird. Calm but with an underlying note of tension he had never heard before. "Are you listening?"

"Lucas? What's going on? How did you get on this channel?" And even as he said it, he felt a small thrill of success. The Light Wire. The Light Wire was up and running.

"Dad, I've—I have something for you. For everyone."

"What?" Clark was confused. "Look, you have to get off of this line right now, I-"

"Just listen," his son interrupted. "Just—listen to what I have to say. You know I've never been good at talking or articulating out loud but I'm going to try." He took a breath on the other end and Clark could feel the tension. "I had a whole thing written out. A manifesto. I sent it to all of the news stations but I had also planned on reading it right here and now. I'm not going to do that."

"What are you saying?" Clark asked. He had no idea what this was about but he could feel a cold pit forming in his stomach. Whatever it was, he wasn't going to like it.

"All I want to say is—I love you. You haven't exactly been there for us—for mom and me or my brothers—but you tried, and I appreciate it. That's just it though: you actually tried. One of the most powerful men in the universe and you tried and still—it's just not enough. None of it's enough. There's still pain and anguish and hatred and it's become incredibly clear over the last few years that none of that can be defeated. None of it can be destroyed. At best, we can hold it at bay but it always wins in the end. Any seed of happiness is always smothered out by darkness. No matter what happens, we still die. Every sun still burns out. This whole thing is just one big doomed mistake heading towards an inevitable death, so I'm here to get it over with."

"Get what over with?" Clark asked. He could already see the men around the room begin to tense. Everyone in here had been trained in both diplomacy and hostage negotiation as a part of their occupancy training, and they knew what textbook desperation sounded like. None of them knew what to do, but Clark watched one of his commanders give him a hard and questioning look.

"*Trace it*," Clark mouthed and the man hurried quickly out of the room.

And then, as if reading his father's mind, Lucas said, "I know what I sound like, Dad. I know that you're probably trying to trace the signal but there's no need. Right now, I'm hooked into the manual override port on the Light Wire on Lydia. I've got my comm device hooked up to my long-wave receiver and—and it's already too late."

"Look Lucas, whatever you are about to do, you don't have to do it. We've got everything in hand here right now and I can come home and you and your mom and I can talk about this. Just-"

"No," Lucas snapped, a thread of steel in his voice. "It's over. Humanity's cancerous actions are over. We are obviously some mistake of nature—some disease or mutation—because we don't act in accordance with it at all. Maybe the world is doomed and maybe everything is born to burn and die, but we're the only ones who make it worse. We're the only species that makes others suffer. And the only one that suffers itself. As far as I can tell, mother nature tried to wipe us off the face of existence once with the Dislocation and failed. Now we're worse than ever so we need something more. A plague. An extinction. We need to do to ourselves what she could not."

"Lucas, I don't—"

"Goodbye, dad. I hope you go quick." Then, his voice flattening, "You will all bow one way or the other to the Crimson Coronach. And sooner or later, everyone will become a member of the Inflamed."

And with that, there was an audible click from the other end. At first, Clark thought that his son had turned whatever communication device he was using off. Then, as sound began to filter through the speakers, it became clear that he had switched to his manual input channel.

It was like nothing Clark had ever heard before. Still overcome by the emotion in his son's voice, the song that was coming together in his earpiece almost sounded like an extension of himself. The music wasn't exactly music as he understood it, but there was no other way to describe it. It was mournful and at the same time, guttural and organic, as if it was being pumped through some secret throat that mankind had never seen before or had the capacity to fathom. It was a gulping and grinding sound with an achingly slow melody being scraped over the top of it.

Before he knew what was happening, Clark felt the sting of hot tears in his eyes. He almost couldn't bear to listen anymore. The sound was verging on the point of pain and he suddenly yanked out his earpiece along with everyone else, and that's when he realized the problem.

The sound wasn't coming through the earpiece.

It had been so hard to tell at first because the song sounded like it was coming from the inside of his own head like some vivid hallucination, but now that there was no other explanation he knew the truth: the sound was coming through the Light Wire. Had to be.

The golden veins of light that ran up and down the wire were now a throbbing ultraviolet. The mechanism almost seemed to strain with it and with each throb, the color grew more intense.

"Turn it off!" Clark yelled, turning toward the counsel where Nathan, the man who had engaged the Light Wire, was hurriedly typing away.

"I'm trying," the man stammered. "I keep trying to shut it down but the source has been hijacked."

"From where?"

Nathan punched the keyboard a couple of times, then: "Unknown. The signal source is unknown."

"Unknown?" Clark said. "What the fuck does that mean? No where is *unknown*. Every Light Wire in the universe is known. That's the goddam point." But Nathan just shrugged, panic plain on his face.

Suddenly, the music seemed to crescendo, and as it did, the veins of color on the spire pulsed brilliantly, sending out a pulse wave of sound and color. Clark felt it rip through him, like a burst of electricity. It damn near knocked him to the ground, but at the last minute, he planted his feet and righted himself.

"What the fuck was that?" he bellowed. Some of his soldiers had fallen to the floor and were staggering back to their feet. The music had ceased but there was something in the air. Some feeling of anticipation.

It was a few seconds before they heard the sound, and for a few seconds after that, they couldn't identify it. All Clark knew was that somewhere deep down inside of him there were alarm bells going off.

Then he reached hesitantly down and picked up his earpiece. Afraid to put it in, he glanced around the room and saw fear and apprehension on the faces of all of his soldiers. He didn't want to, but he knew he had to do it—

knew that his place as a leader was to do the thing that everyone else was afraid to. So he did.

With a quick and practiced motion, Minister of Defense Seamus Clark popped his earpiece into his ear and listened to the rest of his forces all trying to chime in at once.

They were screaming.

10

THE INFLAMED

Every nerve in Raquel's body crackled as the song played and the pulse wave hit. It was agonizing, and the moment Raquel heard it, she knew something bad was on its way. It had sounded like the Infinite Communion she had heard back aboard the Leopold when 49 had hacked their comms and pumped it over their speakers. It was like a song but not, its tempo and pacing sounding grossly inhuman. It sounded like death itself—like an invitation.

The Infinite Communion had also had the power to bend the hearts of the hopeless toward its abhorrent design. When one submitted to it, the unknowable flicker of the human soul was suddenly snubbed out and replaced with something else. The flesh and bones were suddenly recoded into something horrid, picking and choosing which flesh was worthy and which wasn't.

49 had later explained that he had experimented with death and necromancy, trying to find the perfect form. He had killed and rewrote the code of genes and biology, shaping copy after copy of his horrible creations, and once

he finally landed on a few consistent forms, he had been surprised that the ones that resonated with him weren't necessarily designed for fitness but were some sort of dark and twisted joke.

The monsters the crew of the Leopold had fought were lumbering wretched things with half of their parts removed and rearranged. Humanoids with eyestalks and pelvises for heads. Crawling spiders with ribs and finger bones for legs. They were less like animals and more like pieces of crude and satirical art. Raquel didn't know much about art, but it had felt like the rough and on-the-nose drawings of a misanthropic child who hated their parents. The sort of thing designed only to degrade and destroy.

That was almost what this new song sounded like, but there was something different about it. It was still blunt and brutal but with an underlying depth. It moved the listener in ways they couldn't explain, however sick it made them feel. Raquel almost wanted to stop to try to pick apart exactly what it was about the song that touched her and moved her—what buried ghost of a memory it stirred deep down inside of her.

But there was no time for that now. Now there was only time for one thing. Survival.

When the song reached its climax, there seemed to be a sort of pulse that shot out over the ground. Raquel felt the tiny hairs on the back of her neck tingle as she rocked with the wave, and some people felt more than that as they were knocked sideways into the live wire fence. The crowds in all of the cages were rocking and yelping with the shocks, which is why it took them a moment to realize what was happening.

The reason Raquel noticed was that she felt the blood and brains sliding off of her face. At first, it was a relief—the stain of the woman's accidental death being washed away by some unknown force—but then she saw the body.

The lifeless corpse of both the woman and her son rose into the air in unison, their flesh rippling as if there was something moving beneath the skin. Raquel looked down and saw King staring up in amazement, his eyes wide with incomprehension, and then she turned to see the same expression on Byzzie's face.

The whole crowd watched as the dead were raised, twitching and convulsing into the air. The woman's husband even reached out to touch her but upon contact, his fingers sparked with electricity as if he had touched the fence.

What Raquel saw next would haunt her dreams until the day she died.

The bodies of the woman and her son suddenly sucked into themselves like a ball of dough being rolled between two hands. The balls hovered in the air—globules of rippling flesh—and as they did they slowly turned a deep red color. They almost looked like some sort of grotesque water balloons made out of flesh and filled with blood and churning body parts.

Raquel turned and focused on the ball nearest to her inside of the cage. Then it popped.

Six spear-tipped legs suddenly shot out of the center of the quivering mass and skewered multiple people. Raquel barely managed to dodge one of the legs as it sliced over her shoulder. She felt the wet splash of blood on the back of her neck as someone behind her died.

All things considered though, Raquel had gotten lucky. Byzzie on the other hand had a harder time of it.

Raquel watched in shock as Byzantine Jackson took one

of the legs through the joint of her shoulder. The young woman cried out in pain as she reached up to grasp the alien appendage that had skewered her. Then she cried out in sorrow as she looked down and saw her brother Cory lying on the ground.

The young boy lay there in a pool of dark red, the top of his head sliced neatly off. The whole scene was simply too much for Raquel to take in—too much to deal with. She felt her mental grasp slipping, any semblance of hope draining away. People were throwing themselves against the fence in an attempt to escape, the acrid stench of burning flesh and hair scorching the air.

The multitude of serrated legs that had taken a handful of lives within seconds were all joined together in a single ball of writhing crimson flesh. Shiny black eyes peered out from multiple sockets, and a pair of wicked-looking mandibles clacked at the end of a long and pointed snout.

A foot suddenly knocked into the back of Raquel's head as a body was lifted over her and brought to the creature's mouth. Still holding its other victims, the monster greedily shredded the body, taking whole pieces of raw meat down in huge swallowing gulps. Before its meal was even finished, its body lurched and lengthened, a tail shooting out of its back and whipping through the air like a scythe. Its legs remained their original size, tall and narrow. But the head and body of the thing seemed to be having some sort of reaction to what it had just eaten.

The soft, fleshy parts of it had nearly doubled in size, the fresh skin stretching and breaking to reveal a hard maroon shell underneath. Bones snapped and locked into place as its insides rearranged itself at a frightening pace. Then, no more than a minute after the thing had first appeared, it stood towering over the crowd of people, its legs still pinning bodies to the ground, tail making a whistling sound as it cleaved the very air itself.

Then the real massacre began.

Blood and viscera flew as it began stabbing its fore-legs down. Raquel ducked and weaved around them, turning around to pull the still-shocked husband of the murdered woman away from the monster, but as she grasped his wrist she found that that was all she was holding. With a perplexed look on his face, the top half of his abdomen slid apart and fell to the ground. Raquel let go of the amputated hand.

Blood and body parts flew as people were dismembered and cut down. The chaos of the crowd was so great that they wouldn't have noticed an entire fleet of gunships flying overhead. Right now, they were stuck in a literal meat grinder.

It was then that Raquel noticed the monster was letting out a high-pitched feral shriek. So inhuman was the sound that Raquel attributed it to some sort of cry of bloodlust at first, but then, as her wits began to return to her, she recognized it for what it was. Pain.

Then she discerned another cry coming from her left, a cry of rage. No, *cries* of rage. A man and a woman. Raquel sprang into action.

For a brief moment, she caught a glimpse of Byzzie and King through the bloody melee. King had one of the creature's legs stuck through the top of his thigh, blood running down onto the ground like a river. Despite his wound, he had pulled the creature within range of the electrified fence and was scorching it ceaselessly against a wall of blue sparks and white smoke.

While the monster was weakened, Byzzie was pulling for all she was worth on the monster's tail, trying to mash its body into the fence as well.

In that brief glimpse she was afforded, Raquel knew that they had momentary control of the creature and that they were about to lose it. King was bleeding out onto the ground and visibly losing strength by the second, and with Byzzie's injured shoulder, she wasn't even pulling half of what she normally could.

Fighting against the swinging arms and legs of the crowd around her, Raquel burst towards her two crewmates. She tripped once, stumbling forward and then stumbling again, but was able to right herself each time and before she knew it, she was right next to Byzzie, her hands wrapped tightly around the monster's tail.

She pulled at the same time Byzzie pulled but it wasn't enough. The thing was too big. Too strong. In moments it would be able to shake them loose and then it would kill them. Out of options, Raquel reached up with her left hand and wound her forearm around the thick and fleshy tail as if it were a massive rope. Byzzie pulled and Raquel leaned back with her. They rocked together once, twice, three times, and then on the fourth, they felt the thing's legs shift and stumble and suddenly its body was hissing and crackling against the fence.

Sparks and smoke filled the open area, almost making Raquel gag. Still, the three of them held fast, pressing the flailing creature against the electrified wires. If nothing else, maybe they could short out the circuits and make the whole fence grid go down. If that happened, then at least some of the prisoners might be able to escape up and over the tops of their cages while their captors were preoccupied.

And preoccupied they were; Raquel had no doubt about that. Even in the intense close-quarters struggle, she acknowledged the sounds of shouts and gunfire coming from not-so-far-away. The dead bodies of both the woman and her son seemed to have been affected by the shockwave that had surged through the city, and if that were the case for *every* person that had been killed in the last few hours then the PUC definitely had a fight on their hands.

She didn't know where the other monster was that had been created by the son's body, but Raquel guessed that it had run off in search of easier prey. With the exception of the cage that she was in, the electrified prison that the PUC had hastily thrown up around the city and shoved everyone into was probably protecting them for the most part. At least, until those things ran out of PUC soldiers to kill. Then who knew what would happen to the prisoners. Surely the monsters could jump, and given the ferocity of the one they currently had pressed up against the fence, she doubted they would care too much about getting a momentary shock in the process.

Raquel screamed as she poured every ounce of strength and effort she had left into keeping the monster at bay. She looked over and saw that King's strength was beginning to fail and that Byzzie was practically hanging onto the leg with her single working arm. The electricity was clearly hurting the creature but she wasn't sure it was killing it. As the trio's strength dwindled, Raquel could almost feel the rigid leg she was grasping begin to tense.

She must not have been the only one to sense it, because all of a sudden there were bodies next to hers grabbing the legs, pushing the monster. Blood-streaked faces filled her vision as the other prisoners—some she recognized as Byzzie's siblings, others she didn't—joined them in the effort. Three of its legs dug into the ground for support while two others were being held firm by the people trying to kill it. Using its only free leg, it stabbed out at its attackers.

Raquel squeezed her eyes shut and continued to push, not wanting to know if its efforts had struck home on anyone trying to approach it.

The stink and heat of all those bodies pressing against her felt like some sort of heaven. For the first time since their capture, these citizens were united in fighting back. Not scattered. Not panicking. But acting as one. Avenging their fallen. Defending their home.

And just when Raquel wasn't sure they'd be able to hold any longer, the air was pierced by the burst of an energy rifle. The weapon fired again and again in tight controlled bursts and it never even occurred to Raquel that it might be PUC soldiers. At this point, it didn't even matter, so long as the monster died.

The massive six-legged creature that had caused so much destruction in such a short amount of time shrieked in agony as the energy rounds blasted it apart. And although she couldn't see it happening through the press of bodies and the cloud of smoke that surrounded her, Raquel felt the glorious spatter of the thing's blood rain down on her. The thrashing body suddenly tensed and then began to relax in her arms. Still not wanting to let go, fatigue brought her slumping to the ground along with the weaponized leg, and finally, there was nothing but the sounds of heavy breathing and quiet sobbing.

There was a metallic clack, and the body of the creature abruptly fell back out of the cage as the door was opened. Afraid to look up and see weapons leveled at her, Raquel had to fight her nerves to see who had opened the door.

With a long rifle in one hand and a cylindrical key-like object in the other, 49 stood there among the wreckage like some metal angel, gleaming and deadly in the brilliant sunlight.

"We need to get out of here now," said the android, and before Raquel could even get to her feet two more of the creatures were bursting out of the tree-line.

———

WHEN 49 HAD ESCAPED his captors, he knew that his only real chance to turn the tide against the PUC would be by freeing prisoners. And to do that, he needed a key. As he was being walked down the street, he had seen a few soldiers walk by with what looked like cell keys dangling from their belts. The problem was, he wasn't sure if the ones the soldiers carried could open *all* of the cells or just one. Chances were good that the PUC had assigned different squads to different cell blocks, and in doing so, assigned them all different keys with the hopes of minimizing the chances of what 49 was currently trying to do. If everyone had keys to everywhere, the possibility of a full-blown prisoner uprising was almost guaranteed. But, by assigning them all different cells with different keys, it ensured that if one of the soldiers was killed and his key fell into the wrong hands, they would still only have to deal with four or five cells worth of prisoners at most rather than all of Glenhold and its surrounding areas.

It was a good plan, but 49 knew enough about the PUC at this point to understand one thing: they needed to be in control. No way they would trust a bunch of individual keys to a bunch of individual squads *only*. It simply wasn't in their nature. There had to be at least one master key. Probably a few. The person leading the entire attack would probably have one plus at least one other person in charge of prisoner management.

That person had been Rear Admiral Jeannine Davis and

she had gone down like a bag of rocks before she even knew what was happening. 49 had gotten as close as he could to the two soldiers that the rear admiral was standing in front of, and then rushed in to take them out with three quick firm blows. He had moved with lightning speed, but even so, the last soldier to go down had his rifle raised and was almost able to get a shot off before the android's metal hand clobbered him upside the head.

There were more soldiers inside along with what were sure to be some pretty deadly prisoners, but 49 wasn't sure he'd be able to deal with them all at once. So instead, he quickly reached down, grabbed the master key from around the Rear Admiral's waist, stole both of the soldiers' rifles, and then bolted into the woods before anyone saw him.

He ran toward the city and began to free what prisoners he could so long as he didn't have to walk through an entire platoon of soldiers to do so. He took a few patrols out and ushered as many groups of prisoners into the woods as he could.

Then, just as he was spotted by a passing patrol and they began trading energy bolts, the pulse wave hit.

"Take this," 49 said without preamble as he chucked Raquel a spare energy rifle. "You get King to his feet and I'll grab the captain."

"Wait," Raquel shouted, still lying exhausted on the ground. She felt frozen. Half of the crew was injured. Monsters were roaming the streets. She had just watched multiple people torn apart in front of her eyes. All of this was horrid and paralyzing in its own way, but none of it was what gave her pause. What froze her in place was that look the android had given her as he saved her from falling to her death back at the Jackson home. A knowing look. A look of something fierce and hateful.

She didn't know what it meant, but the idea that this person—this monster—was about to pick up Ritz while he was at his most vulnerable seemed to root her body right to the ground where it had collapsed.

She tried to explain it. Tried to ask. But what could she say? How could she question him? Not only had 49 saved her from that collapsing building, but he had just saved her again not ten seconds ago. Still, there was that feeling in her gut. The unease of an animal seeing hatred in its purest form.

"We have to go," King said, struggling up to his feet.

Remembering where they were and what was happening, Raquel began to do the same as a loud cracking sound erupted from off to their left.

Two of the monsters suddenly blasted out of the forest in a spray of snapping brush and branches. If Raquel thought the one in the cage had been fast and agile then these were practically moving at lightspeed. Her training taking over, she brought her weapon up and fired. The gun bucked against her wounded shoulder, sending hot rivers of pain down her arm and through her chest. The burst of energy bolts cut the leg off of one of the approaching creatures, sending it stumbling to the ground. 49 brought the other one down with a few well-placed shots to its crab-like head. He then began to approach it firing again and again, the creature's legs kicking in the air as it thrashed and died.

Meanwhile, the one Raquel had shot was back up and moving. And even though it seemed slower now, it wasn't moving slow enough. People were pouring out and around her as she struggled to close the distance with the monster, but they kept running into her line of fire. Suddenly, the wounded creature lashed out at 49 and sent a spiked arm through the android's chest, his robe billowing out with the blow.

Liquid golden light sprayed out of the android's back as he was pierced. He didn't moan or cry out, he simply stood there, shocked as if he didn't know he could be wounded in such a way. To be honest, Raquel hadn't even been sure he *could* be hurt. She wasn't sure exactly what would happen if someone were to try and damage him—maybe it would be like trying to stab an automobile engine—but the idea that he had something akin to blood stopped her in her tracks.

Recovering quickly, 49's arm snapped up and latched onto the arm of the creature as it tried to pull it back out. It then pivoted to use its other forearm but before it could, 49 raised his energy rifle and fired a long burst into its face. Black blood and pieces of its hard outer shell blasted in every direction as the monster's head and body were shredded apart. And when 49 had finally finished firing, there was no doubt that it was dead.

"Gosh, are you ok?" Byzzie said as she approached him, holding her own wounded shoulder. She wore an expression that seemed to be closer to amazement than worry.

"I'm fine," 49 said, reaching up to tentatively prod at his wound, and as he did Raquel could already see the silver fibers around his chest beginning to spread over the hole. "I think...I think I'm going to be ok."

"Does it hurt?" Byzzie asked.

"It does," 49 replied, as if realizing it for the first time. Then, snapping out of it, "Go see to your family, Byzzie. Some of those people are in a lot worse shape than I am."

And he was right, Raquel suddenly realized as she turned around. At least three of Byzzie's siblings lay dead on the ground from the first creature's attack and the fact of it hit Raquel all at once, almost forcing her to her knees. Two boys and a girl, including Cory, the young boy who had helped make room for King as he tried to save Ritz's life.

He was by far the youngest of the fallen Jackson children. One of them was a girl around the age of 17, the other boy being maybe a year older. Raquel didn't know the names of either. Trying to hold back tears as she turned away from the bodies, she saw Byzzie standing there, still looking at 49's wound.

Raquel was shocked. Was she more interested in the mechanics of this android than her very own flesh and blood? She didn't even *like* 49. The whole scene was completely incomprehensible, but as Raquel stepped forward to confront Byzzie about it, a hand clamped down on her arm.

Whirling around, she found King standing there with a look of pain and sorrow on his face. His shirt was tattered and soaked in blood. He was leaning against the side of the turned-off fence and it looked like every ounce of energy had drained out of him.

"Don't," he said quietly. He shifted his weight and almost lost his balance. He may have even fallen down right there if Raquel hadn't rushed in to catch him.

"Don't," he repeated. She planted her feet and hoisted him up, his arm wrapped tightly around her shoulder. "She can't deal with it right now."

"What?" Raquel asked, confused.

"She can't process-" King nodded back in the direction of Byzzie's dead siblings, "-*that*. And to be honest, we can't afford the time. We need to find a ship and get the hell out of here or Ritz is going to die. Us too, probably. We need to leave."

As cold as it sounded, he was right. Ritz was still laying on the ground suffering from multiple gunshot wounds. Half of the Leopold seemed to be injured in one way or another. And they were currently in charge of more than half a dozen kids with God-knew-how-many of those monsters running around.

They needed to leave.

———

Vanessa Jackson pulled herself up out of sleep and into a world of pain.

Her head was pounding. Her chest ached. Fire seemed to dance down her side with every breath. But still, she was alive. It was surprising and she couldn't exactly understand why they hadn't just executed her on the spot. Then, as she slowly rolled over, careful not to draw attention to herself, she understood.

Men were running around, shouting into the radios on their shoulders. Apparently, the Light Wire had done something. From what she could gather from the frantic chatter, the wire had emitted a pulse that transformed dead flesh into living monsters.

A deep and vivid ultra-violet emanated from the Light Wire's spire and bathed the huge room in a purplish glow. Minister Clark himself seemed to be shocked into immobility, leaning against the platform where Vanessa had tried to wrench his gun away.

The most shocking thing however—the most unexpected and surprising part of the whole scene was the thing on the roof.

High above, crawling over the transparent bulletproof glass ceiling was a creature unlike anything Vanessa had ever seen. With thin legs and a hard carapace shell, it looked like some sort of ant crossed with a crab. Desia had many creatures in both of those species groups, but none like this. This thing looked cold and alien. Less like an animal and more like a shadow given a hard material edge. She was transfixed by it.

As she watched, she saw another appear from the south side of the building and then two more from the west. Before she knew it there were at least seven of the crab monsters on the transparent roof. What was more was that she seemed to be the only one in the room to notice. Everyone was frantic and focused on their comms.

"Hey," Vanessa tried to shout, pointing up at the ceiling. Pain clenched her sides and smothered the warning so she tried again. "*Hey,*" she managed a little louder, pointing up at the ceiling.

The only one who noticed was Seamus Clark. Looking over at her curled up on the floor, Clark saw her as if noticing her for the first time. In fact, the look he gave her was comparable to how someone might address an unwanted insect that had somehow found its way into the house.

"Look," Vanessa begged, still pointing. She felt as if she had about a tenth of her normal lung capacity and her voice reflected it.

Clark wasn't hearing it. Pushing off of the platform, he strode slowly over to her, unclipping the strap at the top of his holster. Rage and disgust alternated in his expression. There was a light scuffing sound of metal on leather as he drew his weapon.

"Up there," Vanessa cried, forcing the words out. Each syllable was another kick in the ribs. The words did nothing however. She could have been speaking gibberish for all the effect they had. Clark kept approaching, slowly lifting the gun until he was mere feet away and the barrel was aimed directly at her head.

It looked like he was searching for something to say—some final words to deliver before killing her. Anguish roiled on his face and for a second Vanessa was convinced that she actually was the source of whatever was going on. His finger began to tense on the trigger.

"What the fuck is that?" Someone yelled.

The words themselves probably wouldn't have been enough to save her. What saved her—at least for the time being—was the fact that all of these men and women had been hearing the screams of their friends and comrades dying over the comm system for the last fifteen minutes. With no decipherable words or explanation, the only flow of information they had been receiving were the cries of pain being pumped over their radio frequencies.

And when they finally laid eyes on the culprits, whose appearance struck some deep and primal chord of disgust on all who saw them, it only took one of them to break. After that, all was lost.

Before Clark could recognize what was happening, one of his soldiers had brought his rifle to his shoulder and unleashed a torrent of energy bolts at the ceiling. There was the sound of air being ripped apart by the burst as ten deep gouges stitched across the bulletproof glass.

"Hold your fire," Clark bellowed, suddenly turning away from Vanessa. There was a brief moment of silence as the soldier who had fired stared uncomprehendingly at the monster, now obscured by damaged glass.

Then the creature began thumping its strange-looking legs down on the ceiling. It struck with one leg, then two at once. There was a furious clicking sound as others raced to its position and then began doing the same, alternating between beating on the glass and digging at it with what looked like a sharp pair of pincers.

"Will this glass hold?" Clark asked. Everyone had their guns up and were aiming at the spot where the creatures were congregated and no one seemed willing to respond. "Will it *hold*?" Clark asked again, turning towards Nathan, the man behind the computer counsel.

"Uh, yeah," the man stuttered. "That glass is military-grade. It should be able to stand up to .50 caliber machine-gun rounds."

And, as far as Vanessa could tell, it was holding up. The initial burst of energy rifle fire had put a few deep nicks into it and a few scratches were appearing as the things tried to dig their way in, but if the glass was anything like what was used onboard the space vessels she had commanded then it would take weeks for them to dig through.

The glass held. The doors, however, didn't.

———

AFTER TAKING off in the Leopold and ditching the bodies of the dead and unconscious SEUs, Kit and Nadia had skimmed low along the tree-line away from the city and then slowly looped back, all while attempting to stay out of radar range. They made a couple passes at the city but each time they did they had to either dodge patrolling gunships or they received a red warning light on their counsel that let them know they had been detected by radar. Each time they were forced to either discreetly back off or outmaneuver any gunships that were dispatched upon their detection.

They monitored the radio channels the crew typically used but they were silent. Then after the pulse wave hit, every channel was flooded with cries for help. Furiously flipping from channel to channel, Kit heard an endless torrent of soldiers begging for assistance, punctuated by screams of pain. His heart was heavy with the sheer amount of death. The PUC invasion had been bad enough, but this...

When shit hit the fan, they were able to cruise closer and closer to the city, and then they finally saw what the problem was.

In a small clearing near the edge of town, almost twenty PUC soldiers were crouched in the center trying to set up barricades. They were using everything from barbed wire to small vehicles in a furious attempt to set up some sort of perimeter. And before they were even close to being finished, Kit watched with a sickening feeling growing in his stomach as a massive wave of what looked like some sort of giant insects crashed over the desperate soldiers. Some of the monsters appeared to be cut down by gunfire, but the sheer speed and number of them ensured that the tiny PUC force was overwhelmed in less than twenty-seconds.

"Swinging around," Nadia said from the pilot's side of the small bridge. With the seat having been removed for 49, she had to stand hunched over the counsel with the magnetic boots of her armor engaged to make sure she didn't slide sideways or fall.

The ship made a tight turn and then cruised back around to make a pass at the clearing to see if they could offer some fire support, but by the time they were lined up, everyone was already dead and the monsters were fleeing.

"I think some of them are dragging bodies," Nadia said.

"What? Why?"

"Don't know. Looks like they're heading to the center of the city though."

"Can we get close enough to get a lock on them?" Kit asked, the ship's ballistic system already queued up.

"Not yet," Nadia responded. "We'll have to wait until we get closer to the city where things open up. The jungle canopy is too dense here."

"What about all those gunships we were seeing? Where are they?"

"I think some of them bugged out back to the carriers in orbit. Couldn't be all of them though. I swear there were-"

An array of red flashing lights suddenly blared on the counsel as they felt the ship rock sideways.

"What the fuck was that?" Nadia said, bracing herself.

Before Kit could answer, something big and red crawled across the viewport.

"What the fuck was *that*?" Nadia repeated.

"I think we've got company," Kit said, pulling up the side-cams that ran along the ship. All across their hull were huge insectoid creatures. And though he couldn't say for sure, he thought that they looked different from the ones they had seen on the ground. These were bulkier with larger bodies and they only had four legs where the others had six.

"Banking," Nadia said as she hit the accelerator and banked hard to the right. The maneuver was fast and jarring and Kit saw one of the creatures lose its grip and fall off the side. Then, to his amazement, he watched as two pairs of transparent wings rose off of its back and it swung around, continuing to pursue the ship.

"Hold on," Kit said, queuing up multiple locks on the ship's ballistic system. "I think we're in for a helluva ride here."

11

DEFENSES

"I saw a medical center this way," 49 said as he led the bedraggled group of prisoners into the center of town. He had a rifle slung over his shoulder and was carrying Ritz in his arms, careful to keep him on his side. "I'm sure they're packed to the gills right now but it's our best chance at saving Ritz's life."

The idea made sense to Raquel but it also seemed incredibly dangerous. If the monsters were created from dead flesh, then surely a medical facility would have been ground zero for an initial breakout.

"What about the Leopold?" King asked, the words coming out clipped and saturated with barely concealed pain. With his arm slung around Raquel's shoulder, the two had developed a sort of staggered limping rhythm as they walked.

"I've been trying to hail the ship ever since we were captured but they're not responding."

"Ever since we were *captured*?" King said incredulously. "You got a radio built into your head or something?"

"Yes, actually," the android responded. "It was essential

in letting me control my own minions aboard the Mary. I used it to transmit a constant signal that let me reorganize dead flesh."

"Speaking of which," Byzzie interrupted, "Just what the fuck are these things?"

"They don't have a name," 49 replied, "But you can call them Necrosarks. They are dead things. Inanimate flesh rewoven by Void energy. All you need to know is that they eat and kill and that's it. They are a truly invasive species and if their spread is left unchecked they will kill every living thing in the universe. Period."

"How do you know this?" Byzzie asked. "Have you seen these things before?"

"No," he replied. "No one has ever seen these before. But I recognize the pattern. The behavior. Their goal isn't to survive like other animals, it's to kill. Something from the Void must have ridden on the back of the Light Wire signal."

"So you're saying if we shut down the Light Wire, we stop these things?"

"Theoretically."

"It worked with you."

At this, 49 looked over at the young woman. Byzzie was battered and bruised, crusted blood mixing with sweat on her skin and clothes. She had just had her home invaded by not one but two invading forces and lost family members in the process. By all accounts, she should have been a sobbing heap on the ground, not throwing verbal jabs at the android that had just saved her.

Everything considered, Raquel wasn't sure her demeanor was a good thing.

"Again," 49 said after a second of consideration, "theoretically."

"Stop!" Someone suddenly shouted from in front of

them. 49 was blocking Raquel's line of sight, but two men dressed in civilian clothing emerged from buildings on the left and right sides of the street, each of them holding energy rifles. Raquel would have bet there were more of them that she couldn't see.

"This man needs help," 49 said firmly. He didn't need to gesture at the unconscious body he had cradled in his arms. "He's been shot."

"Shot?" Said the man in front. He stepped around to the side and as he did Raquel saw that he was an older gentleman with charcoal skin and a white head of hair. He held a large black pistol in his right hand; it was pointed at the ground but out of its holster nonetheless. "*Shot* is as lucky as you can dare hope for right now. I got men and women inside with their guts hanging out. Most won't last the night."

"If this man doesn't receive medical attention soon, I doubt he'll last another 30 minutes."

The man seemed to roll that over in his mind. Then, with a jerk of his head, he motioned for 49 to come inside. "Just you two," he said. "Anyone else who's injured can line up right here." He pointed at the ground just outside the door. "We have a few beds and even fewer medical staff. Most of 'em are...well, this is a backup facility mainly for storing supplies. The actual clinic down the street is somewhere you really don't want to go right now."

"Are you a doctor?" 49 asked as he stepped through the doorway.

By the time the man answered, they were out of sight. But Raquel heard the answer clear enough.

"I'm the janitor."

With King still hanging on her shoulder, Raquel looked around and thought about their current location. The supply building was dug into the side of a row of other two-story structures in the middle of a long straightaway. It wasn't necessarily a defendable area but it could have been worse. A few of Byzzie's injured siblings—along with a couple strangers they had been imprisoned with—had started lining up to have their injuries looked at.

"Hey, why don't we get out of the street," Raquel said, raising her voice and letting more than a hint of unease creep in. Then to King, "Why don't you hop in line?"

"Let them go first," he said. "I've had worse."

"Line up alongside the building," Raquel heard Byzzie say. It seemed as if she too was reluctant to get in line before her brothers and sisters did.

"Bullshit," Raquel said. "I could probably fit my whole hand in that hole."

"I'd appreciate it if you didn't."

The people did as they were asked, lining up single file to have their injuries looked at. The armed men who had come out remained where they were, looking nervously up and down the streets. Raquel scanned the windows in the nearby buildings and was able to spot more than a few barrels sticking out.

"At least go lean up against a wall," she said. "I'm not exactly looking forward to dragging you down the street when we're ass-deep in neck sharks or whatever the hell 49 called those things."

"That I can do," King said, easing his arm off of her shoulder. "Just don't forget about me if I pass out."

"I don't think anyone should be passing out just yet," Byzzie said, walking over to the two of them. Her gaze was fixed on something over Raquel's shoulder.

"Ah shit," King said, still hobbling over to the wall. "Can't get a fucking break."

Raquel unslung her rifle as she turned to look behind her. She had been expecting to see a wave of monsters skittering towards them but what she actually saw may have been worse.

Walking four abreast was no less than thirty armed PUC soldiers coming down the street.

It was clear that they had seen some action recently but by the looks of it they all had working arms and legs. Raquel glanced at the armed men on either side of the street and saw them step back into the shadows.

She nodded at them, gripping the handle of her rifle. The troops were about 200 feet away now and Raquel turned to face them.

WOOD AND METAL splintered as the doors to the spire room blew inward. Everyone had been so focused on the monsters above them that no one was prepared when five of them exploded into the room from the main hallway, immediately cutting down three of the soldiers who had been standing within range.

Vanessa leaped to her feet as fire and chaos erupted around her. Pushing the pain to the back of her mind, she dove behind the pulsing spire, and as she did the severed limbs of at least two soldiers followed her along with a shower of fresh blood.

The screams of men and women mixed with the alien shrieks of the creatures as both human and monster died. Curling up into a ball, Vanessa gathered herself, her mind racing as she tried to find a way out.

A burst of rifle fire came from just around the edge of the structure Vanessa was hiding behind, followed by the boots of a woman walking backward as she emptied her magazine. Frozen in place, Vanessa watched as the soldier pulled the trigger again and again. Before the gun clicked dry however, two serrated legs suddenly pierced the woman's abdomen and she cried out, blood gushing from her mouth.

Before she could think about what she was doing, Vanessa raced forward and yanked the dying woman's sidearm from her holster. The monster tried to hoist its kill into the air so it could stab out with one of its other legs, but before it could, Vanessa dropped into a shooting stance, flipped the handgun's safety off, and drilled nine rounds into the thing's insectoid face.

The creature fell backward gurgling and thrashing as the woman had, and as it did, Vanessa reached up and pulled the soldier away.

The woman's face was pale, dead eyes staring up at the ceiling. Pushing away any feelings of remorse for the moment, Vanessa stuffed the pistol into her waistband, quickly searched the body, and came up with two fresh energy rifle magazines.

The urge to look around her was incredibly strong, but she knew if one of the things were closing in on her she wouldn't be able to outrun it. Now was her only chance to arm herself and escape and if she didn't take it she was as good as dead.

More bursts of gunfire erupted around her along with the *pock-pock-pock* of a handgun. The noise was deafening though not nearly as deafening as it had been 20 seconds ago. Vanessa picked up her pace, ejecting the nearly-empty mag from the rifle and slamming a new one home. She pulled the bolt, felt the weapon hum to life in her hand, and then snapped it up to her shoulder.

One second later and she wouldn't have made it.

Just as the front sight of the rifle lined up with the rear one, the snarled shape of one of the creatures skittered into view. Its face was streaked in black blood and it was missing at least two of its limbs. For all the damage it appeared to have taken though, it still moved with frightening speed. Its beady eyes quickly locked onto Vanessa and it sprinted forwards.

The gun pounded against her shoulder as a spray of blue energy bolts sawed the thing's body in two. The creature recoiled with the hits, stumbled backward, and then its left side fell away from its right with a sickening wet squelch.

Before she could celebrate, she heard a shriek come from the other side of the spire. Quickly sidestepping around it, she fired two bursts at another one as it sliced a retreating man in half. Most of the rounds went wide, but two or three hit home, sending it reeling.

Feeling as if she had spent too much time in one place, Vanessa turned to run. The smashed doorway was less than 50 feet away at this point and as far as she could tell, the path was clear of both PUC soldiers and the insectoid creatures.

She took two running steps forward and nearly tripped over a body. Stumbling to a halt, she threw a quick glance behind her and almost stopped.

Minister Clark was forcing himself to his knees, eyes staring at the ground. In his left hand was his sidearm, the slide locked back in the empty position. The gun shook noticeably in his hand and as he tried to stand, Vanessa watched as his intestines spilled out of a deep wound in his lower abdomen like a bundle of grey fisherman's ropes.

Seeming not to notice, Seamus Clark turned to look at

her. His eyes were cold, his lips tight. He wore the same expression he had worn not minutes ago as he had approached her and raised his gun to her head. She was nothing. A bug. A barrier between him and his ultimate goal.

She turned and ran, leaving him to die.

———

"Don't shoot."

The man who gave the order was tall and grim-looking. He was close enough now for Raquel to make out the criss-crossing of scars on his arms and face. She had seen the pattern before and recognized it. At some point in his life, the man had been tortured by a militia group. Probably Kingsbane.

"Are you talking to my soldiers or yours?" Raquel said, her voice steel.

"All of them," the man replied. He had been carrying a rifle but he deliberately slung it over his back. "I'm calling for a ceasefire. No one else needs to get shot today."

"Yeah?" A voice called from one of the building's windows. "And are you gonna leave too? Or do you plan on sticking around to stand trial for all of the war crimes you've committed since you arrived?"

The PUC commander hesitated. "Let's deal with what's in front of us first."

"What do you propose?" Raquel said hastily, making sure an argument didn't erupt. The last thing she needed right now was to be caught in a firefight standing in the middle of an open street.

"Most of the creatures are regrouping. We saw it as we

passed the medical center. They'll be coming soon though. I think we should be ready to meet them."

Raquel found that she didn't exactly disagree. "What do you mean by 'regrouping?'" She asked, trying to buy time to think.

The man started walking forward, gesturing for his men to do the same. Raquel winced, expecting gunfire to rain down from the rooftops at any second. She saw a few of the shadows in the windows above her sway nervously, but they held their fire. The man stretched his hand out when he reached Raquel.

"Colonel Hutchens," he said.

She took it carefully with hers and shook. "Raquel Fisher."

Hutchens nodded. "Raquel Fisher, I don't know what these things are, but I know they don't care what side we're on. I'm here on a job and as far as I can tell, that job has gone belly-up in a big way. Now, not everyone I landed with feels the same way—or *didn't* land with," he said rolling his eyes. "Most of the brass still up in orbit are confused why we're not all back home already eating dinner with our families."

"And what do you think about that?" Raquel asked.

"I think they can come down here and see for themselves." Hutchens straightened up. "Now you asked me what I meant by 'regrouping.' I don't know exactly what these bug-eyed bastards are doing, but I know they've pulled back and I know they're congregating near the medical facility. I've been in a lot of fights and I know what regrouping looks like. So believe me when I say this: we're about to be going toe-to-toe with those things. And I don't mean *a few* of them."

Then, as if on queue there was a shout from one of the windows.

"They're coming!"

"Shit," both Raquel and Hutchens said in unison, facing opposite directions. Each of them spun around in turn to see the advancing horde coming from both ends of the street.

The army of monsters looked less like an invading force and more like a hurricane of long knife-edged limbs. They crawled over the ground and the buildings and even each other. The sight stirred something wretched in Raquel and she felt herself involuntarily gag. There was something about the way they moved. Like a swarm of insects.

The people waiting in line to have their injuries assessed were now trying to funnel through the tiny door without trampling each other to death. King had limped to the entrance and was ushering them through, making sure they made it inside safely.

"Raquel! C'mon!" Byzzie yelled over her shoulder as she ran to follow her brothers and sisters.

Energy bolts gushed from the windows in blue and green streaks of light. Some of the creatures were cut down but immediately replaced by three more. They moved so fast up the street that Hutchens' platoon almost didn't have time to react. Almost.

"Opposing firing formation," cried Hutchens as his soldiers raced to their positions. Groups of seven and eight soldiers lined up kneeling on the ground while another seven to eight stood standing behind them. One of the formations faced the creatures coming from the east and another faced them from the west. Almost as soon as the last soldier had taken up position, Hutchens yelled, "Fire!"

The standard PUC energy rifle carried 50 rounds and a

single magazine could be exhausted in just under three-seconds of continuous fire. The soldiers were disciplined however, even in the face of certain death. Running to the door, Raquel watched as the standing soldiers opened up on the incoming horde with tight, well-aimed bursts, making every shot count.

Then about four-seconds later, the kneeling soldiers began to fire as well. At first, Raquel didn't understand why, but soon the soldiers who had started shooting first began to run empty and reload. They conducted the motions almost like machines. When a soldier ran dry, they would quickly eject the mag, drop it on the ground in front of them, and then replace it with a fresh one. The whole procedure took under three-seconds, and the staggered fire made it so that there was a wave of blue pulverizing death constantly blanketing the field of fire.

The Necrosarks screamed and died as they advanced but they didn't slow.

Raquel was standing in the doorway now, rifle gripped in her sweaty hands. She had been in battles before but never one of this scope. From what she could tell, nearly fifty of the creatures had to have been killed or wounded by this point. Hutchens' platoon stood firm, their shoulders almost touching, but she would have bet good money that they were frightened beyond belief.

"C'mon," Byzzie yelled again, yanking Raquel's shirt. "We have to get inside."

Raquel turned to follow, but as she did, a shadow suddenly appeared above them. Without another thought, she spun and fired, knocking a Necrosark off of the side of the wall just above them. The creature screeched and thrashed to the ground between Raquel and Byzzie and more than a few soldiers spun their heads to look behind them. Raquel pumped round after round from her energy rifle into the thing and was joined by Hutchens coming up beside her. Finally, with a shudder, the Necrosark died.

Raquel looked up to see Byzzie crouching wide-eyed in the doorway, flecks of black blood on her face and arms. She stood back up and said, "I think I need to go find a gun."

Just then, a loud scrabbling sound could be heard coming from the roofs above them. Raquel and Hutchens both snapped their heads up and then threw a glance at each other.

"You need to pull your men back," Raquel said urgently.

Hutchens looked reluctant to do so, but then he looked down at the dead body of the monster that had fallen to the ground in front of the doorway and gave a decisive nod. "Fall back, on me," he barked, reaching down to pull the dead thing out of the way. Raquel stepped closer and helped kick it to the side.

"Byzzie, tell the others to watch the entrance to the roof," Raquel yelled over the gunfire. "I think they're pretty focused on us right now, but they could be coming in any second."

Byzzie nodded and darted back into the building.

They pulled back not a second too soon. The Necrosarks were mere feet away, lashing out with their legs and pincers. The soldiers fired as they retreated, but even so, the monsters doubled their efforts to push in on their prey. Raquel watched as they began throwing themselves forward, their weaponized limbs puncturing men and women even as they themselves died.

Raquel fired over the heads of the retreating soldiers, trying to keep track of her ammunition. She had spent probably fifteen rounds on the Necrosark she had killed with Hutchens. She had been firing in a nearly blind panic and now had less ammunition than she could have had if she had been thinking. Nothing she could do about that now though. She had switched her rifle to single-fire and was trying to aim carefully for the things' heads and bodies. They were small targets in comparison to the reach they had with their legs, but she found that a few well-placed shots usually slowed one down, even if it didn't immediately kill it.

Two creatures skittered up the wall on the opposite side of the street and Raquel saw one of the Desian men lean out and knock one off with a burst of fire as it passed. The other one turned to pursue the man and Raquel swung her rifle and squeezed off a quick pair of shots. The first one went between two of its legs, but the second hit it square in the back, causing it to lose its footing and tumble to the ground.

The retreating soldiers were almost inside now but at least eight of them lay dead in the street where they had been cut down. Their deaths had bought the others valuable time but the losses were huge. Just over 2/3 of Hutchens' original force now remained.

"Go, go, get inside!" The commander yelled as the last soldier staggered backward, still firing her weapon. The creatures were virtually in their faces now, lunging forward against the combined fire from Hutchens' and Raquel's rifles.

One of the creature's legs speared through the air just over Raquel's head as she pumped three rounds into its face and body. Three more were already closing in and Hutchens suddenly reached over and shoved Raquel backward through the doorway. She stumbled and fell to the ground on her side, barely managing to hold onto her weapon. And before she could get back up, she recoiled as a serrated leg punched through Hutchens' abdomen.

Raquel pushed herself back to her feet, stepped around Hutchens and shot the first attacking creature. It screamed and died and she pivoted to shoot the other one, pulled the trigger and heard the tell-tale click of an empty magazine. Wasting no time, she slung the rifle over her shoulder, grabbed Hutchens by the arms and pulled him inside just as a pair of pincers snapped the air where his head had been half a second ago. The creature rushed in and Raquel dropped the man to the floor and smashed the metal door closed in the thing's face.

People were already running up beside her as the door took a beating from the other side, rattling on its heavy hinges.

"That's not going to hold for long," said a voice Raquel recognized and she turned to see 49. Two women she didn't recognize were also there, checking Hutchens' wounds and then lifting him onto a stretcher. "Come on in. I think we found our ticket out of here."

12

———

TERMINAL

It took everything inside of Vanessa to keep from bolting away into the jungle. The monsters behind her had been terrible and every muscle and instinct urged her to get away from them as fast as she could. With a herculean effort, however, she was able to convince herself to stay inside of the building and try to find the administration office.

It took a few minutes of looking—she ran quickly and quietly from room to room—hoping desperately to avoid any living thing that could possibly be in there—but when she eventually found it, it had exactly what she was looking for: a comm-system.

The built-in receiver had a boosted signal that most likely had ground-to-orbit transmission range, and as Vanessa began switching through the channels, she was relieved to find that she could hear the chatter between the orbiting ships.

"This is Light Wire station to all PUC vessels," she said, keying the mic and cutting into a conversation between two ship captains. "Our forces are overwhelmed. Minister Clark is dead. I need a Tesla bombardment on this location ASAP."

"Who is this?" Replied one of the captains.

After a moment's hesitation, Vanessa said. "It doesn't matter. All commanding officers are dead down here. We've been overrun by some sort of insect creature that somehow originated from the Light Wire. We can't shut it down from here so you have to destroy it. Please, I'm begging you."

Vanessa waited for a response. Five seconds passed and she tried again. Nothing.

It was what she was afraid of. They had no idea what the situation on the ground was, and some unauthorized person asking them to destroy the Light Wire—the very reason they were here—seemed an awful lot like something an opportunistic militia member would do.

"Fuck," Vanessa said to no one, pressing her fist against her forehead. She took a deep breath and began trying other channels. Some were dismissive of her claims while others seemed to be dealing with situations of their own. They all blew her off without exception. Some asked for more details than others but the end result was always the same: radio silence.

Then, after about five minutes of flipping through silence, stubborn captains, and panicked distress signals, she came upon someone she might be able to work with.

"Please repeat. Did you say 'destroy the Light Wire?'" said a woman's voice. The signal was clearer and closer than the ones she had been using to talk to the ship captains.

"Yes, I repeat. The energy pulse originated from the Light Wire. If we can destroy it then we might be able to stop these things."

"Coming around for a bombing run," said the voice. "What are your coordinates?"

"They are..." Vanessa quickly looked around the desk that held the receiver she was using until she found what she was looking for. A small foldable map with the current coordinates written in pen in the lower right-hand corner. Someone hadn't felt comfortable uploading them to whatever digital database the PUC had been using down here—not when the facility had been built secretly in enemy territory. She checked and double-checked the coordinates against the map and then fired them off into the handset.

"Coordinates received," the woman said. "Civilian Class Vessel, designation Leopold coming around for a bombing run."

Vanessa felt her heart flutter. *The Leopold.*

"You said the Leopold. Is this—" she frantically searched her mind for names, "Raquel? Nadia?"

"Nadia, ma'am."

"Nadia," she breathed. "Is Byzzie there? Can I speak to her?"

"She's not with us but her location is our next stop."

"Good." Vanessa gave herself a precious moment to breathe. To be thankful.

"Hey, Vanessa?"

"Yes?"

"Get the hell out of there."

"The Leopold is coming to pick us up," 49 said as Raquel followed him into the building. "It just needs to make a quick detour."

"A detour?" Raquel asked.

Looking for Ritz, the two of them made their way into a large room. It was clear that this had once been a storage facility that had hastily been transformed to accommodate patients. The two-story building was open up to the ceiling, providing lots of space for storage racking. All along the sides and down the aisles of the racking were people lying in cots with nurses and doctors sprinting back and forth between them.

"They're going to destroy the Light Core."

"Do you think that'll work?"

"It might," 49 said. "It worked with me."

Making up her mind on the spot, Raquel reached out and grabbed his arm. The android jerked to a stop and spun around.

"Before we go any further," Raquel said, leaning in and speaking quietly. "You tell me right now what this is."

"What do-"

"Cut the shit," Raquel said, trying to keep her temper in check. "This whole thing just absolutely reeks of what you did onboard the Mary." She pulled him in close. "Tell me everything and tell me *now*."

"Raquel, you know everything I know."

"Get fucked," she suddenly shouted, pushing him away from her. The heads of a few nurses snapped around to look at them. Raquel suddenly felt the entire weight of the day pressing down on her. The running and fighting. The killing and death. Image after image of people being impaled or decapitated flashed in a constant reel through her mind. "You know something. I know you do."

49 looked around, a look of comprehension slowly sliding over his face. And there was something else. Something like fear, mixed with resentment.

"See, right there." Raquel said. The muscles in her face twitched and contorted as she fought the urge to cry. "*Right.*

There. You know something. I saw it in the Jackson house and I saw it near the cages."

"What's going on?" Byzzie said, jogging up to them. She had a sling on her arm and a thick pad of bandages where she had been injured.

"This asshole knows something and he's not telling us," Raquel said.

Byzzie's curious demeanor immediately transformed into disgust. "I knew it," she said. She reached down to her hip and pulled out a small pistol Raquel hadn't noticed. She raised it and pressed the barrel up to 49's eye.

"Spill it," she said.

"This isn't the place-" 49 began to say, but Byzzie leaned in, jamming the barrel into his eye and forcing him back.

The android looked around, worry creasing his expression. Then he finally spoke.

"I guess I'm not great at hiding emotions yet," he said, defeat heavy in his voice.

"I guess not," Raquel said flatly.

"That look you saw—back at Byzzie's place and after I freed you—it was hatred."

"Why?" Byzzie said, pressing him. "Because we let you live? Is that it? Because we let you draw breath or whatever it is you do for one moment longer instead of killing you as soon as we could?"

"The hatred isn't for you," 49 responded. "It's for myself."

This stopped them. Raquel didn't know how to respond.

"I felt something when I grabbed your hand, Raquel," 49 continued. "I still don't understand my own anatomy yet. The Light Core, it—it reacts to energy. It's why I could detect the Void's signature on the energy pulse."

"So what does that have to do with anything," Raquel said.

"At the Jackson house, when you fell and I grabbed your hand, I detected something inside of you. A residual effect from when you cracked the Light Core onboard the Leopold and used it as a weapon against me."

"What?" Raquel said, worry edging her voice. "What did you detect?"

A look of pure shame and sadness washed over the android's face. "When you were exposed to the Light Core, you were exposed to high doses of radiation. While you recovered fairly quickly from the initial effects, it was enough to leave you with something called Electron Dislodgement Syndrome."

"What's—what is that?" Raquel asked.

"For all intents and purposes: it's cancer." 49 replied softly.

Then before she could absorb the words, there was a large bang overhead. Everything seemed to freeze and then a number of armed personnel around the warehouse began yelling to each other.

"What's happening?" Byzzie said, looking around.

"I think we're out of time," 49 said.

Raquel tried to focus—tried to figure out what to do next—but all she could hear were 49's words.

Cancer, he had said. *Out of time.*

13

WHAT IT MEANS TO END THE WORLD

"We've got more bugs coming up on our six," Nadia yelled as she dipped and dove through the air. Trying to shake the creatures off, she had banked and rolled the Leopold so many times by this point that she was afraid the nuts and bolts holding it together were about thirty seconds away from popping out.

"On it," Kit responded. The ship shook as the guns along the side fired.

After fighting back the first attack, Nadia had abandoned all notions of stealth and began buzzing the city, looking for activity. Since then, they had fought off four more waves of the things.

Then when it seemed they had finished off the last of them, a massive wave of the creatures descended on the Leopold with all they had.

The ship's ballistics system saved their asses. In their quick zips around the city, they had seen more than a few downed gunships. They had all undoubtedly unleashed the full extent of their firepower on the buzzing horde as they were attacked, but the weapons systems onboard the PUC vessels only had machine guns with a fixed line of fire. They had a locking missile system as well, but the bugs were likely too small and fast for a lock. On top of that, the PUC vessels were bulky and cumbersome compared to the slick maneuverability of the Leopold. So, while the gunships were good at attacking ground targets and other fighters, they must have been virtually helpless when the bugs had attacked.

The Leopold had survived almost strictly on its maneuverability and wide range of fire. No bug stayed on them for more than a few seconds, and therefore had little time to pry their way inside.

In the midst of the fighting, 49's voice had hailed them over the comms and given them something more to do than just fight for their lives. Nadia had then whipped the Leopold around and began heading towards town when Vanessa made contact. Bumping her request up to the top of their priorities, they turned around once again and made their way to the coordinates the Fleet Commander had given them.

"Looks like we've got a full schedule all of sudden," Nadia said as she swung the nose of the ship to the right, still trying to shake the huge bugs off. Ever since the pulse wave had hit it seemed like she was desperately trying to keep the ship in the air. The bugs were strong but hadn't been able to break through the hull yet. What they had been able to do however was bust up some of the nav gear and docking ports. Almost anything on the ship that didn't have a smooth edge had been dinged, dented, or ripped off by this point.

"Nadia, how are we going to destroy the Light Wire?" Kit asked from beside her. "49's gone, which means we can't use the Javelin. And I don't think these machine-guns are going to cut it."

Nadia thought about that for a second and then came up with an idea.

"You still got the Tesla Arc from your Marauder armor?" Every Arc Suit that the SEU's had been given was powered by a small Tesla Arc. They weren't big enough to fly a ship but they might just be big enough to fire a Tesla round: a hyper-condensed bolt of energy that was typically used in ship-to-ship combat and Tesla bombardments.

"Yeah, but it's trashed. What about yours?"

"We need some way to port into the ship. I can connect with my neural drive, but I can't send that much energy through it without spraying my fucking brains all over the computer console."

"So what are you suggesting?" Kit asked.

Nadia pointed at his missing hand.

THE SOUND of energy rifles blared inside the storage facility as Raquel raced to the stairs. The sounds of the creatures banging on the doors could be heard coming from multiple directions now and it seemed like no one knew which entrance to run to.

Judging by the sounds of battle coming from up above them, the people near the roof entrance seemed to be putting up the best defense. The back and front ground-level entrances on the other hand seemed as if they were already fully penetrated. Screams and sporadic gunfire came from either direction and what seemed like an endless wave of people were converging on the middle of the facility.

"Get to the roof," 49 said. "You can hold them off from up there."

"Wait," Byzzie said. She had just finished gathering up her siblings and counting them off. "Where are you going?"

"I'm going to go get Ritz. The Leopold should be here soon and you should be able to take off from the roof. If I'm not there when they come, just leave. I'm in contact with Kit right now so if I get pinned down you can always swing back around and pick us up."

"Sounds like a plan," Raquel said.

"Oh, and Raquel?" 49 said, pausing.

"Yeah?"

"Take care."

"Yeah, you too," Raquel said briskly and turned back toward the stairs. She felt bad about accusing him of being involved in what was going on but she didn't have time to deal with that or anything else she had just heard in the last five minutes. As far as she was concerned, she was going to live for another hundred years and fight like that was the case.

A crash came from nearby and Raquel spun to see a Necrosark burst through a shelf of supplies and impale one of the doctors Raquel had seen running around helping patients.

"Go," 49 said, sprinting in the opposite direction.

Byzzie raised her pistol and fired off a quick three shots at the monster and it recoiled and disappeared back through the shelving.

Feeling suddenly naked without a rifle in her hands, Raquel looked around for something she could defend herself with. What she saw though made her immediately switch her priorities. Not ten feet away was a small elderly woman lying unconscious on a cot with a bandage wrapped around her head. Deciding to forgo a weapon, Raquel sprinted forward and wrapped the woman up in her arms.

When they reached the base of the stairs, King was already trying to hobble up them as people raced by.

"King, I'm going to need you to move a bit faster than that," Byzzie said as she ushered her brothers and sisters past him. The older ones were carrying the smaller ones in their arms, and Raquel's heart broke as she noted the ones who hadn't made it out of the cage.

"Maybe you should carry me," King said, picking up the pace. He was still limping on his injured leg but judging by his slow reactions and demeanor, someone had given him some pretty strong pain meds.

"Move along," Byzzie said, pushing him from behind. Then she turned and handed Raquel her pistol. "Here, watch our backs. There should be about 12 shots left."

Raquel repositioned the unconscious woman in her arms so she was hanging over her shoulder and then reached out and took the gun. "This isn't exactly the ideal fighting stance."

"Yeah well," Byzzie said. "This isn't exactly my ideal visit home."

———

"WE'RE COMING UP ON IT," Kit said.

The jerry-rigging of the Tesla Arc into the Light Wire port had been relatively straightforward. When Byzzie had made Kit's prosthetic limb, she had run a connecting wire from the prosthetic into the Arc Suit. In turn, his hand could be used to port into the ship. So after lugging his smashed armor up onto the bridge, Kit was able to run the Tesla Arc through his armor, through his prosthetic, and into the ship.

"God, I hope this doesn't blow my arm off," he said half to himself.

"If it does, I'm here for ya," Nadia said reassuringly, though when he looked over at her he could see worry plain on her face. This was their one chance though. If they failed this then they failed everything.

Kit gritted his teeth. "Here we go."

———

SEAMUS CLARK FELT like he was swimming. Something warm and wet occupied his lower half and he had the distinct feeling that he was bobbing up and down. He had thrown up once already and most of that had been a dark red color. He looked around the room.

Blood and bodies covered the floor. Slowly, he turned his head, taking in the carnage. No one. Nothing moving. He wondered if he could stand. He looked down at his legs.

They were gone. And not only were they gone, but they were continuing to disappear.

The monster that was bent over his lower half was meticulously chewing on his waist. He couldn't feel it. Couldn't feel anything.

All he felt was some deep well of sadness.

His boy. His beautiful child had done this somehow. Clark wasn't mad or angry. He was just sad that he'd never see his boy again. Never ask him why. Never hear his thoughts. It was over. It was all over.

He turned his head to the side to look at the Light Wire. The throbbing magenta that had originally been there had been replaced by a dark purple. What was more was the metal at the base of the structure. It was gone.

Something was happening to the Light Wire. The spire

itself seemed to be hovering in midair. And in the space between the bottom of the spire and the ground, there was something floating. Some sort of liquid that was just now coalescing into a single tight ball of ebony.

Clark stared and for a second he thought he saw something looking at him out of that deep black ball. There was a glint. An eyeball. It blinked.

Then the Light Wire was engulfed in a ball of blue fire.

———

"THEY'RE COMING!" Raquel yelled as she fired her weapon down the stairs. Stepping backward up them, it was all she could do not to stumble and crush the head of the woman she was holding.

"They're already here!" Byzzie yelled from up ahead where a group of soldiers were firing in the opposite direction. The sounds of the dying were filling the air all around them. Men and women and monsters all screaming in unison. A chorus of death against the backdrop of ripping metal and the electric thrum of energy rifle fire.

They were closing in. And for the hundredth time that day, Raquel felt helpless. It was all too big. The odds too great. The crushing currents of reality smothering her and all the other tiny things as they shifted. If she didn't die now then she'd die later of cancer. She had been faced with the choice to die peacefully or fight hopelessly before and she had chosen to fight hopelessly. She had used the Light Core they had stolen as a weapon and had expected to die while doing it.

In a way, she had.

Time seemed to flow together for her and she wondered what the accumulation of a thousand moments like this might look like. Would it be Hell? If she had experienced that many of them, then surely they made up the majority sum of her life.

And then, with a sickening feeling, she realized that she had been here before.

On the ship, when she had passed out, she had seen this along with a million other horrible and hopeless scenes. They had all played out like a reel and she felt like she had inhabited each and every one of them. It had felt like infinity then. And it felt like infinity now.

One of the Necrosarks clanged up the metal stairs, as fast as if its feet weren't touching anything at all. Raquel fired her weapon once. Twice. Three times.

Then it clicked empty.

———

Vanessa had barely made it clear when what looked like a Tesla round leveled the Light Wire facility. Blue fire and electricity erupted and painted the jungle around her, making her feel as if she had been dipped into the very sky itself.

At some point, the sun had begun to set and the jungle around her had begun to squeeze her with its dark hands. Still, there was enough light from the burning facility to make out the shapes of dead corpses around her. Most of them had the jagged edges of smashed combat synths.

The synths had likely been deployed as soon as the fighting had started and then been cut down along with everyone else. But they weren't the only bodies on the ground. Four or five Desian civilians lay on the forest floor with darkly glistening holes in them made either by energy rifles or the stabbing limbs of the monsters.

Something had happened here.

Whether these people had been killed by the creatures or the PUC, their lives had amounted to the same end. Living breathing human beings with hopes and futures and secrets about themselves that they had yet to unravel. Dead and forgotten out in the jungle.

The scene was so grim that it almost brought her to her knees.

Suddenly, the jungle exploded with purple light. Vanessa swung her head back toward the flattened Light Wire facility and this time she actually did fall to her knees. It was another pulse wave. The song wasn't audible this time but it was there all the same. In her heart and in her bones.

And in the dead bodies that had just begun to lift off of the ground around her.

They had destroyed the Light Wire but it hadn't been enough. Whatever was powering it had forged a connection with this place and no longer needed the machine itself. Another wave would hit and another one would hit after that.

And with it, every dead body would rise up and walk the earth with the serrated limbs of mindless monsters. An endless army sent to transform this and every other world into its own living Hell.

———

Lucas Clark sat in his own Light Wire facility and considered what it meant to end the world.

In his right hand, he held a small .38 revolver that he had taken from his dad's gun cabinet back home. He thumbed the safety off, displaying the tiny red dot indicating it could be fired. He thumbed it back on again. Such a strange thing. A tiny tool designed to throw a little rock through the air. A spark. A bang. Then nothing. Like the big bang but the opposite. An anti-creation.

He had heard the sounds of much larger guns outside and even a few down the hall but still nothing had found him yet in this room.

So this was it. This was his revelation made real. He hadn't expected it to look like this, but he wasn't particularly surprised either. He knew it would be something along these lines. Something...brutal. Something final.

Night had descended overhead and the stars could be seen through the thick bulletproof glass above him. He looked up at them and tried to count. He lost track and started again.

Someday they'd all be gone. Those big and burning lights would flicker out, along with everything else. Nature would have run its course. Billions of species would have lived and died their natural lives without the horrid interference of mankind. And then everything would return to the way it was before. All darkness and black. Nothing.

Same thing with a person. When they died, they would be returned to that infinite blackness, never having known they had existed in the first place. No one to question it. Just simple nonexistence. The most basic and natural state of reality.

It was strange to him that anything even existed at all. Why? Why was there this brief and temporary glimmer of being in the first place? Why not nothing? Forever?

It would be nice returning, he thought to himself. Nice to return back to wherever he was before he was born. No stress. No worrying about finishing assignments or pleasing his parents. No feelings of powerlessness and impotence as he watched the world fall apart through the lens of a computer screen.

Lucas watched as something streaked across the sky overhead. Maybe a comet. Maybe a ship fleeing the planet. Maybe even just an illusion caused by his brain fighting desperately against what he was about to do.

No matter. Nothing could stop it.

Lucas reached up and put the gun beneath his chin, smiling one last time as he thought about the world he had created.

Then he flipped off the light.

THE END

Ash Above, Snow Below

The Omen Tree

ABOUT THE AUTHOR

Fredrick Niles is the author of *Ash Above, Snow Below* and *The Omen Tree*. He lives in St. Paul, Minnesota where he writes fiction, bartends, and sells board games. In his free time he rants about movies, lurks in bookstores, and practices introversion with his wife.

 facebook.com/fredricknilesauthor
 instagram.com/fredrickniles_author